The
Cruel Shadow
of
Love

The
Cruel Shadow
of
Love

C.V. Naveen Reddy

PARTRIDGE

A Penguin Random House Company

To order additional copies of this book, contact
Partridge India
000 800 10062 62
orders.india@partridgepublishing.com

www.partridgepublishing.com/india

To

my sweetest nephew,

Reyansh

A wholehearted thanks to

Nisha Rai

for the creation of this splendidly heart-touching story

Also a hearty thanks to

Hema Maharaul and Tejaswi Pooja

for their sincere and timely help with various aspects

Last but not the least, my deepest thanks to

Deepsikha Tiary,

For the invaluable help of introducing a

meaning and purpose to this book

Contents

The Happy Beginning

WAIT! Are you looking for a book with a happy beginning that has an inevitable happy end? Then you are certainly in the wrong place. Unfortunately this book isn't one of those books with a classical 'lived happily ever after' ending. One obvious reason why I started this book with a WAIT written entirely in capital letters is to give you a fair warning of the nasty things that you would encounter if at all you keep reading, despite my warning.

Trust me—the WAIT at the beginning is not written for sarcasm purpose. People think most writers are very sarcastic, which holds true for a lot of writers. Though many prefer to keep you guessing, I do not. Now that you have a fair idea about the dreadful ending, don't, for the sake of God, blame me for the rolling down of salty teardrops on your sad, sunken cheeks at the end of this book. After all, aren't the more philosophical ones that say 'It is the journey that counts and not the destination itself'.

So, getting back to our story which undoubtedly has a heartbreaking end, this day was indeed very beautiful and pleasant. Everything around was as orderly as usual. Of course any given day would be pleasant, if only you did not come across terrorists who were blowing up your neighbour's building or if all the mangoes in your garden were stolen by the street kids or if your car had a heck of a starting trouble. There could be a thousand reasons why you could not tag your day as beautiful and pleasant.

In the numerous overgrown trees across the street were birds that were chirping their tiny hearts away. It was a day round about the end of February and the beginning of March—the dead of a malevolent winter and the dawn of a new, revitalizing spring. The mighty sun was rising over the horizon, lighting up everything in its way as it rose. The city was painted by the bright golden rays, revealing all that was hidden by the twelve-hour-long darkness. How very usual! Isn't this what the mighty sun been doing for the last five billion years or so? The only change being the change on the landscape. *Sigh.*

Sunday, 4 March 2007

Edy was still leaning on his study table right in front of his bedroom window. On any given day, one could expect the medium-size room to be tidy and arranged, but not today. It was strewn with filthy clothes, bathrobes, bath towels, electronic gadgets, charging equipment, books of grade 10, papers both scribbled and empty, stationery of all kinds, pillow covers of different colours and sizes, and a lonely standing acoustic guitar, among various other room belongings.

He was fast asleep now, after having spent one of the most awful nights ever, regretting a series of unpleasant events that had happened a few days ago, the nastiest one happening precisely on 15 February 2007. Those sinful events almost looked like they had been taken out and enacted from a well-scripted, perfectly plotted romantic-mystery book.

The tears which had rolled down his sunken cheeks had created a fist-size pool on the marbled floor and still the last pain-filled drop hung at the bottom edge of the table.

In his wounded heart he well knew he was going to lose someone who had become excessively indispensable to him, someone that he cared for, someone that he couldn't bear to live without, someone who had a profound influence on his life like no other. He was willing to do anything in order not to lose someone that he well knew he was going to lose and he was more willing to go to any extreme to set things right—things that would only be set right if time itself could be turned backwards. The thought of 'nothing can be done now' was terrifically unbearable for him.

What was even more disturbing were the diabolic thoughts of his new-made enemies, who majorly contributed a large chunk to what led to all the mayhem. The handful of people and the recent conversion of their evil thoughts into iniquitous acts were the key cause for many things that had horribly gone wrong.

As the sun rose higher and higher, it lit up all the strewn rubbish in the room, including Edy's depression-filled face. Both his lifeless hands were rested on the damp tabletop. His right cheek pressed hard against the wet wood. His palms were slackly covering two tiny objects, small enough to be hidden in his cup-shaped palms, which were facing the tabletop. He had held on to them all night long. The two unlucky objects were not even supposed to be with him—not, at least, after 14 February 2007.

The sun had now raised enough to pass its rays into the tiny gaps between his fingers that dimly lit up the two unfortunate objects. A mixture of dark red, bright white, and shiny black could be seen through his sunlit finger gaps. The other object was vaguely visible and it looked like something made out of paper, but a lot more thick and solid. Neither did it shine nor have a bright covering.

'Edy, wake up, honey,' a soft but firm voice floated from behind the locked door, following a few gentle knocks.

'It's almost thirty past eight now,' the caring voice continued. 'You do not want to be late today, do you?'

The gentle door knocks grew louder.

Edy jerked, holding the two objects more firmly as he abruptly woke up from his shallow sleep. The brisk movement disturbed the still-hanging teardrop, which was now wobbling. His swollen eyelids opened only to reveal a colour that was redder than the object that he had held. As he stared at the painted wall to his left, he realized how miserable his life had become in the past few weeks.

All the unexpected twists and turns that had taken place in his school flashed before his grief-struck eyes. Most of the frightening ones had happened only days ago. A strong memory of an unforgettable handshake, the fragrance of the winter flowers from the church garden, the contents of an ill-fated diary were the first things that his brain could recollect from his memory drive.

The very first emotion that ran down his spine as he recollected the events was the sudden burst of a mixture of sadness, anger, agony, and fear—fear of all the terrible past as well as the dreadful events that were about to take place in a month's time.

His 'morning sadness' syndrome, or MSS for short, had only gotten worse. Yes, 'morning sadness' syndrome—the sudden feeling of an exploding ball of negativity deep inside due to a recent emotional activity that one experiences as he/she wakes up in the morning. It only occurs to those who have had a bad emotional past or to those who know that something dreadful is going to take place in the near future.

'Mark, please wake up Edy. Breakfast isn't ready yet.' Edy heard his mom's faint voice ebbing away from the room door.

'I'm on it, he'll be up any moment now.' Edy's dad spoke as he walked up to the door. 'Edy, Edy, wake up,' his dad called out, gently tapping on the locked door.

The knocks disturbed him further, which forced him to reply to the calls. 'Yes, Dad, I'm up,' Edy spoke, still not moving from his sitting-leaning positing. The voice was deep, husky, sleepy, and rough.

'Oh, good, I thought so,' Edy's dad said. 'Would you want me to help you with the packing?'

'No, but thanks, Dad.'

'Okay, son, I'll wait for you downstairs,' his dad said and went back to reading his morning daily.

Edy gently felt the two objects that he had held on to and gradually raised his heavy head and turned towards the objects. His left cheek rested on the half-dried table. All that he could see was darkness, both literally and figuratively. The strong rays of the sun temporarily blinded Edy's vision. His heavy eyelids dropped down momentarily before they opened up, flickering as they readjusted to the blinding yellow rays. His vision was still half blurred and the background was getting brighter with every passing minute.

His clumsy hands revealed the hidden contents. He had seen them a hundred times before, and every time he saw them, his mind had a hundred thoughts popping up and loitering about in his two-pound brain. As he stared at the red-white-black coloured object, all he could see were the words inscribed on it, 'Loving Is More Fulfilling Than Being Loved'.

As the words passed through his thought-filled mind, he, for the first time, began to think about them. Taking a deep breath, he shut his eyes again, which took him to a whole new world and at a much different time. The wobbling teardrop detached itself from the slimy edge and splashed noiselessly on the drying pool.

Sunday, 4 June 2006

It was the beginning of June and Edy knew he had to quit his lazy home life and get back to his lovely boarding school, for this would be the most important year of his academic career. Edy, as described by his close friends, was affable, companionable, and ever jovial. His strong ability to abstain himself from getting under the spotlight for a bad reason was a natural boon. Such was his strong grasp on his valiant thoughts that no outside element could ruffle his immense dedication and moral attitude towards academics, cleanliness, integrity, and righteousness.

It was the tenth grade, the first turning point of any school student. Edy would be passing out of high school within a year and undoubtedly any grade 10 student would be serious about the year ahead, as was Edy.

The wooden cuckoo chimed as the clock hand struck nine. Edy had already finished his morning routine of bath and breakfast and took a final glimpse at the elegantly arranged room to remember if he had forgotten anything useful, because he knew he would not come home for the next five months or so. His sharp deductive eyes carefully scanned every tiny object that was lying around. As he assured himself, he held on to the cylindrical handle of the huge black suitcase and dragged it along through the room door.

'Done?' Edy's dad asked as he stood at the entrance, adjusting his white collar.

'Yes, Dad,' Edy swiftly replied.

'Let's get going then,' Edy's dad said as he buttoned his sleeve while his mom adjusted the red tie.

Edy gave one last look at his house as he loaded the large black suitcase into the car's boot space. All the three sat comfortably and buckled their safety belts. The engine grunted as the rpm needle scored along the rpm meter. The RJ on the radio continued to play the top 40 list. They quickly reached Highway 377/B and the car picked up speed as Edy's dad pushed the accelerator hard against the floor. The three occupants were all geared up for the four-hour-long drive.

'Are you sure you did not take any electronic gadgets with you, honey?' Edy's mom said as she turned the radio volume down. 'We do not want any more complaints on you.'

'No, Mom,' Edy said, busily fiddling with his dad's phone. 'I left them back at home.'

'Are you sure?' Edy's mom spoke as she turned back to him. 'It's not Mr Fieldson who's the principal anymore. The rejoining letter stated that the management bought in Mr Joseph Matthew as the new principal.'

'So?' Edy asked, still looking at the phone screen.

'Going by his years of experience, his qualifications, and the serious testimonies from various institutions, I don't think you'll be lucky enough to get off with a warning, in case you happened to sneak in anything that is prohibited,' Edy's mom reminded him, sounding a bit more serious than before.

Edy raised his head; his eyes looked concerned.

'And I happened to read about him on the Internet.' Edy's mom revealed, 'He seems to be a very stern character.'

'He's going to be fine, honey,' Edy's dad interrupted, still keeping his eyes on the road.

'I know he's going to be fine, Mark,' Edy's mom said with a smile. 'It's just a mother's instinct to be concerned about her child—'

'Right,' Edy's dad said, shifting to a higher gear.

After four hours of travelling, they could finally see the school compound at a distance. Within minutes, the car entered the gates of Morey's Public School. Edy's heart gloomed. It was his third consecutive year at MPS. One of the reasons that made his boarding life much easier was that he absolutely knew everyone at MPS and almost everyone absolutely knew Edy, unlike the new students joining the school, who had a bit of a problem making new friends.

'Finally, heaven on earth, Mom,' Edy said as he jumped out of the car. The refreshing cool breeze ruffled through his hair. The sight of lush green trees dominated the grounds of MPS. Soon a dozen of his old friends gathered around the Ravenden family.

'Edy, how are you?' an excited voice spoke as another friend joined the small group.

'Barrie!' Edy exclaimed loudly, eager to meet his best pal.

After a quick conversation with the Ravenden family, the polite friends helped Edy with his rather heavy luggage.

Soon, Edy's mom and dad were back in the car, buckling their safety belts.

'Take care, Edy,' Edy's mom said as she waved him goodbye.

'Take care, son,' Edy's dad joined in.

'I will. Love you, Mom, Dad,' Edy said, waving his goodbye. Barrie waved too. 'Bye, Mrs Ravenden.'

The engine roared again and soon they were driving out of the gates of MPS. Both Edy and his best pal Barrie chattered away as they headed towards the senior boys' dormitories.

The next morning all the four-hundred-odd students, both new and old, were dressed in school uniform, attending their first school assembly. The first day of the new academic year was more refreshing than the following three hundred days. The colour of school uniform of green and cream dominated the assembly ground, blending with the huge, lush rain trees that were spread over the enormous grounds of MPS. The cross-striped green-and-white tie added a little trend to the old-fashioned school uniform. A majority of the students had brand new black leather shoes that shone with added polish and an extra bit of shine from the shoeshiners.

Edy and Barrie had their first glimpse of Mr Joseph Matthew, along with the three hundred and ninety-eight curious pupils. His strict expression was strongly conspicuous. He did not show even the slightest expression of a smile—not even the *s* of *smile*. He was dressed like a military official, clean and tidy; his shoes were shinier than any student's.

He had thick, short grey hair and was probably in his fifties. His belly slightly bulged out from the metal buckle. He looked like he had been in a principal's post for at least twenty years. Probably that was the reason behind his slightly oversized belly.

'So what do you think?' Edy murmured as he stood in a line that belonged to grade 10.

'He seems to be nice,' Barrie whispered, sarcastically.

No, Edy thought as he took a closer look.

The new principal stood next to the tall wooden podium on the cemented stage and examined the uniformed mob ahead of him, like a robot trying to find a faulty machine parts.

Mom was right, Edy thought as he saw the authoritarian and ruthless look on his face. *He's a very stern character.*

The first assembly commenced with the school choir singing the first of the two school anthems, upon the school captain's command. Edy felt like he had only been out of the school for a week, though it had been almost two months. No major change had taken place, except for the change of principal, and a few newcomers, both teachers and students.

Mr Joseph's uncanny eloquence was completely hidden until he made his first decorous speech. The first speech—the welcome speech by the principal—came to an end with a warning about the outcomes for those who did not obey the rules and regulations of the institution.

Then came the first of the three hundred to four hundred speeches that were supposed to be delivered in the school assembly, one each day. Most of them were by students, who gave motivational speeches to keep the spirit of the students going strong. Others were more story-based, the stories and events that were successful, apparently after a lot of struggling by famous people from history.

As a familiar face stood behind the podium to deliver his the first inspirational speech, most of the senior mob knew the exact motive behind the speaker's wish to deliver the first speech on the first day. Any other student would only try and escape from delivering the first speech.

'Look,' Barrie whispered to his pal, 'Ivan Anderson delivering the first speech.'

Now there are only two reasons why one would deliberately point at a particular person, especially in a place like a school or college or office or any other place where lot of people come together every day. One is if he/she is exceptionally good at something, say, like a rock star or a movie star. Two is he/she is awfully bad at something, like scoring marks or at playing soccer. Fortunately or unfortunately, the speaker, Ivan Anderson, strangely fell into both the categories.

Ivan Anderson, a grade 10 student, was more prominent among the school's population for the bad reason. His attitude towards the girls in the school was not particularly very delightful. He was the only student in MPS who perpetually fell in love with random girls every spring or so. Many who knew him tagged him as lecherous. He had the finest collection of opening statements that he unleashed upon his gullible victims. Of course, attached to those impressive opening statements was his tall, fair, and athletically built physique that took care of the mesmerizing part and his light-bluish cat eyes that created the rest of the charming effect. All together he was one mean magnetic machine that lured all the innocent victims into his list of 'She's been with me'.

'I wonder which unfortunate girl is destined to fall into his traps this year.' Edy sighed.

'Certainly a newcomer.' Barrie sighed too.

'And an awful lot of new faces,' Edy muttered as he swayed his eyes from corner to corner.

'Yes, I see them,' Barrie swiftly replied as he turned and looked across different aisles of different grades.

'Look at that one in grade 9,' Edy said amusingly, pointing his eyes at a newcomer who was constantly gazing at the enormous trees.

'Tourists,' Barrie said, giggling.

'Yeah, we'll see them at least for the next two months,' Edy commented.

'That's so unsympathetic of you both,' said a friendly senior who stood in the grade 11 aisle. 'You should have seen yourselves when you both were new a few years ago.'

'Oh, Terry, please,' Barrie dimly said, 'the rite of passage continues, we're just having fun with the new ones.'

As the fair magnetic machine's speech ended, Mr Joseph Matthew, who was a stern character, took some time to introduce the new faculty members. The new additions included Mr Grey Garrison (the new boys' dormitory warden), Mr Sam Fisher (the new physical training teacher), Mr Coogy Cal (the new music teacher— well, actually the new violin teacher as he only taught violin). Mr Joseph Matthew, soon after introducing the 'violin expert only', assured the students that they would soon recruit another music teacher to help with all the other instruments.

The first assembly ended with the school choir singing the second school anthem followed by the more patriotic national anthem. All the students marched back to their respective classes in queues that resembled marching fire ants.

Miss Andrella, who was handling English for the senior boys, was appointed the class coordinator of grade 10 for the ongoing academic year. As she entered grade 10's classroom, she could see quite a lot of new faces. Crammed with lots of boys and girls, the classroom showcased vast diversity that filled the air. Some were tall, some short, some fair, some wheatish, some pretty, some vicious looking, some content, some confused, some happy, yet some annoyed, thanks to their school uniforms that made them look uniform.

The clock struck nine and the first bell of the school day went off. All the loitering students now occupied their respective seats. Miss Andrella made her way to the front and stood on the mini cemented dais.

'Good morning Miss Andrella,' all the students greeted her in a tone that sounded more like a lullaby.

'A very good morning to you all,' Miss Andrella wished with a broad smile on her bright face.

She continued to speak with her loud, very loud, voice that echoed the large hall.

'Today being the first day and the first class,' she continued, 'let us all take the time to introduce ourselves.' Most of them knew this was coming. It was the usual opening statement of all the teachers at the start of a new academic year.

'As most of you know, my name is Andrella and I handle English for the senior grades.' She continued, boastfully, 'I am appointed as the coordinator for grade 10 for this academic year.'

She swayed her head from side to side and glanced at the large uniformed mob from under her spectacles. 'Now I want you all to introduce yourself to your class,' she said, 'and please keep it short and simple.' She stopped and sat on the swirly chair.

Edy, who was seated at the extreme left of the first row, stood up to introduce himself. 'Hello, everyone, I'm Edy and this is my third year at MPS,' he said, looking at the gazing audience of forty-seven, 'and my hobbies include reading books, mostly novels of action and mystery, and love to play soccer, baseball and water polo among various others. .'

Miss Andrella nodded, having heard of Edy's unchanged hobbies for the last three years. Barrie, who was seated next to Edy, stood up next.

'Hi, I'm Barrie and this is my sixth consecutive year in this school.' Barrie continued as his palms became sweaty,

'And I love riding bikes and . . . um . . . dancing is another favourite hobby of mine.'

Miss Andrella gave a 'we all know you very well' smile.

'Phew, that was some hard introduction,' Barrie said with a sigh. He hated it when many eyes stared at him, especially the new pairs of eyes. 'Finally done introducing myself for the sixth time,' he said as he wiped his sweaty palms on his thighs.

Allen, a guy who could be described by words like *peevish*, *argumentative*, and ever *irascible*, was seated right behind Edy. He was probably the thinnest of all the grade 10 students. His body weight did not seem like it belonged to a grade 10 student. A grade 7 class would be his ideal competition ground. He had a pointy nose, pointy jaws, pointy hair, and pointy black leather shoes. The first thing that anyone would notice about him was his thick, powerful, proportionally large spectacles, without which he would practically turn blind. He was mostly known for his humorous comments on others, and most of the time, it pissed off his victims.

Allen stood up, adjusting his heavy spectacles. 'Hi, I'm Allen Weirton and I have been in this school for eight years.'

Eight of the ten newcomers put on a shocked expression; their jaws dropped and eyebrows rose. He was undoubtedly the oldest student of grade 10 and one of the oldest students in MPS.

'And I love horse riding—that's the only hobby that I embrace the most,' he said.

'Yeah, Allen, we all know how much you love horses—shut it,' Edy murmured, turning back. He was only making Allen taste his own medicine, to give him a feel of how it felt when someone made humorous comments.

Miss Andrella did not quite seem to be as shocked as the new students. She was one of the oldest teachers too. She knew Allen from when he was a kid.

Celia, who was next to Allen, stood up. 'Hello, I'm Celia,' she said, her charming voice grabbing the attention of the new boys. 'I have been here for the last three years and my hobbies include playing violin, swimming, and also abstract painting.'

'Yeah, right,' Barrie whispered to his companion, 'you should listen to her play the violin.'

'Don't be ridiculous,' Edy bounced back. 'She's still a beginner.'

'She's been learning to play for almost a year now,' Barrie said, wickedly giggling.

'I know, but we never had a good violin teacher, remember?' Edy said, referring to Mr Murray, the previous music teacher who was very bad at teaching violin.

'You're so mean,' Celia, who had overheard the conversation, whispered as she learned forward towards Barrie.

'No, I'm not, honey,' Barrie said, covering his mouth with his palm. 'I was only explaining to Edy how beautifully you play the violin.'

'Zip it, meanie, I heard it all,' Celia said, annoyed.

'And just for the record, she's the reason why Mr Murray lost his job,' Barrie said to Edy.

Celia punched Barrie hard on his shoulder. 'You know there were fourteen others with me,' she whined. 'And Mr Murray deserved it.'

'Okay, Miss Violinist, I agree with you,' Barrie said, rubbing his shoulders.

'Oh, would you both stop it, enough already,' Edy whined, annoyed with Barrie's silly comments and Celia's defensive statements.

'Quiet there,' Miss Andrella said, in a loud voice that overpowered the voice of the student who was introducing himself. She stared at Edy, Barrie, and Celia momentarily before returning her frightening gaze towards the introducer.

As the introduction process moved on, the infamous Ivan Anderson's chance turned up. 'Hello, everyone, my name is Ivan, Ivan Anderson,' he spoke trying to sound more like a famous movie star.

'Yeah, right, Ivan, Ivan the "Lecherous Devil"' Allen, one of the many haters of Ivan Anderson let out his first humorous comment to his little group. Edy, Barrie, and Celia smiled, instantly realizing what Allen had meant by the words 'Lecherous Devil'.

'Look at all the new girls, staring at him already, mesmerized by his false innocent looks,' Edy said, and his group turned back to look at the potential victims of Ivan Anderson.

Mable, who was seated adjacent to Celia, overheard Edy's comments. She leaned sideways and said, 'They'll be mesmerized by his looks only until they find out his idiotic lecherous attitude.'

'True that!' Celia continued, 'And all those pricy, exotic things that he gifts just to impress them.'

'Poor, innocent girls,' Allen joined the pointless conversation. 'Why don't you both warn the new ones about his fictitious promises?'

'Allen, please,' Mable sighed. 'Experience is the best teacher, and do we look so jobless to you?'

'Like they would ever believe us,' Celia said as the last student stood up to introduce herself.

'Exactly,' Mable spoke, leaning towards Celia again. 'You do remember what happened when I tried to warn Florentina the previous year, don't you?'

'I remember,' Allen said, giggling hard, at the same time trying to control his giggle. 'She thought you were jealous of her beauty.'

'I know, but eventually she realized his true colour when he deliberately dumped her, poor girl,' Mable said.

'Maybe she will warn the new ones,' said Edy, who now seemed to be interested in the topic of discussion.

'Oh, she's least bothered.' Mable said, 'Why would she care to share her past and make a fool out of herself?'

Allen, Celia, Barrie, and Edy nodded in agreement as they heard Mable's realistic explanation.

'Now that we are done here,' Miss Andrella spoke as the introduction process drove to an end. 'Mr Joseph Matthew will have a quick meeting with us.'

Everyone's attention was drawn to Miss Andrella's loud voice.

'Also he will be here to announce the class representative or CR for grade 10,' she said and looked into the file that she had bought along.

'Before I go fetch our principal, I have an important announcement, particularly for the newcomers,' she said and stood up to have a clearer view of the enormous class.

'Not again,' whispered Rodney, who was seated behind Allen.

'I don't know how many of you have been in a boarding school before,' she said. 'If you have, then you probably know that students don't necessarily have to carry their books back to the dormitories at the end of each day,' she said. Most of the new students paid attention to what Miss Andrella was saying.

'You can leave behind all your books, stationery, and other class materials in the space provided to you below your respective desks,' she continued with her irritating husky voice. 'Hope you all know this is the standard procedure in most of the boarding schools.' Some of the newcomers nodded while others blankly stared.

'If and only if necessary will you be carrying your books back to your hostels, say, when you have exams.' She said, 'You might want to burn a few extra hours on your preparations post-dinner.'

Miss Andrella exited the class soon after her announcement. Gossip began to erupt from the many groups that were formed in grade 10.

The First Benchers included Edy, Barrie, Allen, Celia, and Mable. The 'Up to No Good' group included Eric Reez, Ray, Jeoff, and Morvin. The Seriously Studious group included Wenda Alexander, Veranna, Reny, and Sylvia. The Great Gossipers group included Rochelle, Reeda Melinda, and Margretta. The 'We Don't Care What' group included Joe, Ryan, Benn, and Robin Reeves. Others fell into very distinct individual designations like The Flirter—the infamous Ivan Anderson. The Sleeper was Heith. The Drama Queen was Santana. And the rest were mostly newcomers.

'You won't believe this,' Barrie said as he stared at row 4, desk 3. 'Look, Bonn is back in business already.'

'Hitting on the new ones?' Allen asked, still keeping his pointy head straight.

'What else do you expect from him for the first few weeks?' Edy said as he turned to look at Bonn and the new girl he was talking to.

'And all his attempts go in vain, don't they?' Allen sighed, cleaning his proportionally large spectacles, which he did at least eight times an hour.

'Poor guy,' said Celia, who was trying to show pity on Bonn, 'he's only trying to make new friends.'

'Not to forget his attempts are only with the pretty ones,' Barrie said and Allen put his large spectacles back on.

'Most of the guys are like Bonn,' Celia admitted, smiling as she spoke, 'but he doesn't get lucky enough to bag one.'

'She's a pretty one he's talking to,' Edy said as he stared at row 4, desk 3.

Allen raised his eyebrows.

'What?' Barrie instantaneously asked.

Celia and Allen looked at each other with a 'What did Edy just say?' expression before they looked at Edy. Barrie had his head tilted and a 'Can you repeat what you just said?' look on his face. Edy frowned at the confused onlookers, constantly shifting his gaze at all the three friends. For a brief moment that small part of grade 10 turned utterly noiseless.

Did I do something wrong or did I just say something offensive? Edy thought.

'What's wrong with you guys?' he finally broke the awkward silence. 'I just said she's pretty.'

The three pairs of eyes did not change their expression.

'I think that was the first ever positive comment you have ever made on a girl,' Celia finally spoke, emphasizing on the words *ever* and *girl* a little too much.

'That too on a newcomer,' Barrie said, stressing the word *newcomer*.

'Yes, I guess, so?' said Edy, who now seemed to be baffled at his own comment as much as the other three.

'Okay, this is it,' Allen said, taking his first glimpse at Bonn and the 'pretty' newcomer. 'Edy's attracted to her.'

'What? No, that's ridiculous,' Edy said in an instant, trying to defend himself from being yet another victim of Allen's humorous character. 'It was just a random comment.'

'Comment?' Celia spoke, looking weirdly at Edy. 'It sounded more like praise to me.'

'Oh, come on, Celia, even you?' Edy whined.

'Include me as well,' Barrie said with a funny giggle.

Edy put on a serious expression as he shook his head, the kind of expression he would put on in a heated-up football match. His nose flared up and reddened.

'Do you remember it was a similar kind of comment that led me—' Barrie said, and before he could end the sentence, he was interrupted by a harsh voice.

'No, I don't—that's the end of it,' Edy said, annoyed.

Soon they could hear footsteps erupting from the narrow A-corridor. It was Mr Joseph Matthew, who was a stern character, accompanied by Miss Andrella.

As soon as both entered, all the grade 10 students stood up.

'It's okay, please be seated,' Mr Joseph said as he walked towards the mini dais.

'Thank you,' he said, standing in front of the huge blackboard while some students straightened up their ties. Miss Andrella stood next to the principal. His stern expression seemed a bit eased now.

'Based on the previous year's performance, both academic and co-curricular,' Mr Joseph started, his voice loud and clear, 'I have chosen two student representatives for each class, and both the representatives will perform all the assigned duties without fail.' All the students were keenly listening. This was no time to fool around. Not a word erupted from the forty-eight pupils.

Mr Joseph squinted into the file that he had brought along, while Miss Andrella stood still, with her hands folded.

'The primary representative for grade 10 is—' He paused. The laziest students of the class were listening too for this was a once-in-a-year announcement and not like those recurring announcements by Mr Hal, the computer teacher.

'Edy Ravenden,' Mr Joseph announced.

'What? No!' Edy murmured faintly, shocked, and he jumped up from his desk.

The silent atmosphere was overtaken by loud claps and cheers from the life-filled mob.

Edy quickly went on to the mini dais to receive his metal badge with his name and the words 'Class Representative – Grade 10' inscribed on it. Mr Joseph promptly pinned the prestigious badge onto Edy's chest pocket.

'I hope you'll put up the best of your abilities to perform the task of a representative,' Mr Joseph said, shaking hands with Edy.

'I will do my best, sir,' Edy said not realizing what it would take to perform the tiresome duties of a primary class representative.

The thunderous claps diluted into thin air. Edy went back to his desk with a confused look. He rarely looked more surprised.

'And the secondary representative is—' Mr Joseph paused to look into the file again. 'Wenda Alexander,' he announced. The room was filled with thunderclaps as the second round of applause began.

Wenda Alexander received her own metal badge from the principal. She had more of a proud face than an excited or happy one, and clearly a couple of girls did not appreciate her as much.

'Now before I leave the class,' Mr Joseph said, placing the cardboard file on the table, 'I want to remind you of a few things.' He continued, 'Firstly the seriousness that I expect from you all this academic year is almost unattainable.' He paused.

Miss Andrella nodded in agreement.

'You do realize that this year is the most important year, as you will be passing out of high school in about ten months,' he said.

A large part of the class was trying to resemble the serious look of the principal only to assure him that they were taking his words very seriously.

'All that I expect from grade 10 is academic seriousness,' He sounded even more commanding. 'Ten months of hard work and you'll undeniably pass with flying colours.' He paused again. The only noise that could be heard was from grade 9, which was right behind grade 10. 'Second and almost equally important advice,' Mr Joseph said, 'don't get into unnecessary trouble, especially the kind of troubles that anyone of your age would possibly get into.' He paused with a stubborn look.

At once, the forty-eight students realized what he had precisely meant by that. Some who were already involved in it found it hard to suppress their blushing smiles. That included Barrie and Celia.

'Any involvement in such activities will attract serious action. You can have my word on that.' Mr Joseph couldn't get any more seriousness onto his face; if he had, his eyeballs would only have popped out and bounced on the mini cement dais.

'All the best to each one of you,' Mr Joseph ended and fetched his file to move on to grade 11 and grade 12, to probably give the same advice for the senior grades.

'My God, did the management recruit this man from the military?' Allen asked with a terrified look on his face.

Barrie had sweat drops forming on his warm forehead. 'But what's he going to do without any proof?' Barrie spoke anxiously, as nervous tremors ran down his shivering spine. His voice hardly reached Edy's ears.

'Precisely,' Celia said, trying to calm down her partner. 'How would he ever know about us or anyone else?' A pacified Barrie finally calmed down after hearing Celia, while Edy kept reminding himself what his mom had said about Mr Joseph. He was a very stern character indeed.

* * * * * *

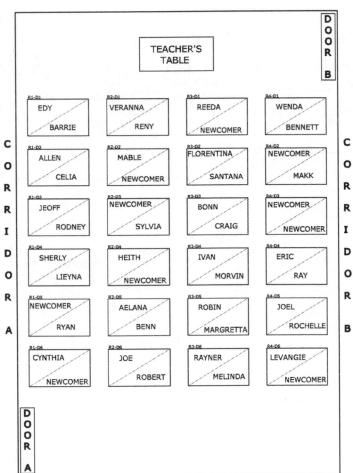

The classroom of grade 10 at the end of day one

The Kingdom of Kutonians

Thursday, 6 July 2006

We humans have been around for thousands of years on this gorgeous blue planet and the one thing that we have been doing for as long as we have been here is keeping a count. Sounds silly, doesn't it? But it's true. Counting is something that has always been an inescapable part of our daily lives and it is also probably the one character among various others that distinguishes us from all the other creatures on this wonderful planet. Be it the number of days left for our next birthday or the amount of money we have saved to buy something nice for someone or the number of miles we have to cover to get to our nearest holidaying spot, the number of vehicles we own, houses, friends, enemies, clothes, shoes, ties, suits, party clothes, the number of likes that our display picture has scored on the social networking sites, the interest due to be paid for our educational loan, the number of people we have dated, the number of people we wanted to date, and whatnot! This is an endless list.

Some crazy people even count the impossible like the number of stars in the night sky or number of hairs on the head. Yet some insane people count silly things such as the number of mangoes that their tree has borne fruit in their backyard or the number of mosquitoes they could successfully smash. It all depends on who you are and what profession you are into—doctors, engineers, postmen, traders, teachers, students, bankers, businessmen, racers, scientists, criminals, policemen, politicians, and authors, to name a few.

Well, authors usually keep a count on the number of pages they could manage to write in a day, among various other things. At least I did keep a count on the number of pages every day, just to make sure I did not miss the pre-fixed release date.

Likewise, back at Morey's Public School, the students too kept a serious count and all that they bothered to count, other than the counting that was required in their math paper, was the number of days. Some made each day count, while others counted to make it through each day, depending on whether the student was studious or not, respectively. Be it the number of days left to the start-of-term exam which took place every three months or so, or be it the number of days left to the end-of-term exam, marking the class calendar was a must. It was not by force but by will.

Someone had already marked out 6 July 2006 on the calendar as Mable leapt forward to do what had already been done. It was she who usually marked the class calendar.

'Ah, great!' Mable said. 'Someone has done the marking already.'

And in a class of forty-eight, there is no telling of who does what, unless the situation is really intimidating and the guilt shows up on his face, in which case you can point your finger at him and say, 'There, he's the one who did it.'

'Thank you, whoever has done it,' Mable said as she turned away from the school calendar, which was hung next to the huge blackboard.

'That would be me,' a familiar voice floated from the end of the class.

'Bonn!' Barrie exclaimed, surprised.

'When did you start to be not so lazy, Bonn?' Edy asked as Bonn made his way to the front desks.

'Maybe from the time he started talking to the pretty newcomer on row 4, desk 3,' Allen commented, cleaning his giant spectacles. Bursts of laughs erupted from the handful who heard Allen.

'No!' Bonn whined, 'She's just a friend.'

'Looks like you have got competition, Bonn,' Edy said, pointing out at row 4, desk 3.

'Ivan Anderson,' Barrie exclaimed as he took a glimpse at Ivan trying out his charming tricks on Bonn's pretty newcomer friend.

'Like I just said, she's just a friend, Edy.' Bonn grunted, being annoyed by the first benchers' comments.

'What about the not-so-pretty one on row 4, desk 2, is she your friend too?' Barrie asked, still giggling.

'Oh no, she doesn't like talking to guys,' Bonn said, looking back at row 4, desk 2.

'She told you that?' Allen asked out of curiosity.

'Ah . . . no.' Bonn paused for a brief moment and spoke again, 'I just assumed she didn't like talking to guys.'

'I thought so,' Allen swiftly reacted.

'Bad Bonn, bad,' Celia commented.

'Now do you get it, why we pick on Bonn so much?' Edy said, looking back at Celia.

'Oh enough already, grow up you guys.' Bonn cried as he headed back to his desk.

'Hope you win against the devil, Bonn.' Allen shouted to make sure Bonn could hear his words, 'To claim your pretty prize.'

Edy, Celia, Barrie, and Mable burst out in laughter.

Soon, the clock struck nine and Miss Andrella entered the class with a bundle of sheets in her file.

'Good morning, Miss Andrella,' the students greeted her.

'A very good morning to you all,' Miss Andrella replied. Her commanding voice did not seem have worn out even a bit.

'What is that bundle in her file?' Barrie whispered.

'I don't know,' Edy said. 'Going by the scary smile on her face, the recent completion of the first unit in English, and the bundle of sheets, I can only assume it to be a surprise test.'

'That can't be true,' Barrie said, frowning.

'Today we have a surprise test,' Miss Andrella finally broke the tension-filled silence, 'on the first chapter, "The Kingdom of Kutonians".'

A large part of the mob instantly changed their expression, half of which largely resembled bafflement and the other half infuriation.

'What the hell?' whispered a faint voice from Rodney, who was at row 1, desk 3.

'Here are the question papers,' Miss Andrella said and started to distribute the bundle, starting from row 1, desk 1.

'The Kingdom of Kutonians?' Barrie asked with a transfixed look right after Miss Andrella strolled towards row 1, desk 3. 'What's that all about?'

'Something about the Kutonian kingdom being attacked by the Westerners,' Edy whispered faintly.

'Right,' Barrie said and read the first question: What was the instant reaction of the Kutonians on enemy's attack?

For a brief moment he thought of the possible answer before giving up. 'What am I supposed to write to that?' Barrie cried, still looking at the first question.

'Shock and disbelief, Barrie,' Edy whispered.

'And what vows did the Kutonians take as the Westerners left their kingdom shattered and torn apart?'

'To invade the enemy territory and strike a deadly blow to the Westerners,' Edy pointed out swiftly.

'That's it?' Barrie whined, 'These questions are for ten points each and your answers will fetch me only about two points.'

'Elaborate it,' Edy whispered again in a harsh, husky voice.

'What are the eminent lessons learnt by both the Kutonians and the Westerners?' Barrie read out the third of the five questions.

'Now no more talking or whispering until everyone has handed the answer sheets to me.' Miss Andrella's deafening voice echoed in the silent hall. She took several strolls around all the four rows, inspecting each one for any unfair practices.

As the class got quieter and quieter, Barrie's heart pounded harder and harder. He did, anyhow, blame the absenteeism of his mind during long and boring lectures, and most of the lectures were long and boring except when it was Miss Ashria Kaum's. All that he could hear was the scratching sound from the nibs that were scribbling on the white empty sheets. Rodney tried hard to peek into Jeoff's answer sheets though he knew Jeoff's answers were no better.

It was almost forty past nine when Barrie had finished answering the first three questions, thanks to Edy's quick reply that saved a lot of thinking time for Barrie. He also managed to attempt the remaining two questions with irrelevant answers, and a ray of satisfaction fell upon his heard as the bells went off just in time.

Miss Andrella kept an eye out for any copyists taking advantage at the last minute as she quickly collected the answer sheets. 'I will distribute all the scored papers before the end of last hour,' Miss Andrella announced and quickly exited the class and entered the staff chambers.

'It's the Vegetable Day,' Allen reminded his weary group of four.

'Damn it, Allen, you had to remind us, didn't you?' Edy grumbled.

'I hate this day and I hate you for reminding us,' Celia followed.

'Lord, save the day,' Mable muttered.

'My day is already ruined,' Barrie sighed, referring to his bad performance in the test. 'It's only going to get worse at lunch.'

'Veggie Thursdays.' Celia grunted. 'Why do you even exist?'

Ever wondered how something as healthy as a few varieties of raw vegetable could possibly ruin your entire Thursday?

Well, the students of MPS did not seem to have much choice about it. They had to, no matter what, gulp down the four to five varieties of uncooked veggies every Thursday afternoon. It was the Chambers of Healthy Dietary's decision. They were very concerned about the diet of the students of MPS. Neither could the students possibly sneak out the bizarrely shaped vegetables from the dining hall nor could they make them vanish using a magic trick. The dining supervisory panel made sure that the much-hated veggies did not end up anywhere but in the rebelling tummies of the students.

As the second bells went off, Mr Hal, the head of the computer department, entered grade 10 with an announcement note. Any official announcement from the Chambers of Principal Authority was conveyed to the students by Mr Hal, not only because he was keen on doing it but also because he was the principal principle conveyer of decisions made at the Chambers of Principal

Authority. Not many announcements that came in from the CPA were particularly very pleasing. Only those that came in favour of the students were appreciated. Thanks to Mr Joseph Matthew, the new stern head of the CPA, who brought about major changes in the school's monotonous routine.

'This is an announcement from the Chambers of Principal Authority,' Mr Hal enchantingly said, holding the note high above his chin.

'Oh please, not again,' Rodney cried, assuming it was just another lousy change that they were about to witness. His assumption was purely based on the previous two announcements, which did not sound so very motivating, one of which was cutting down the evening play hours from two hours to a mere forty-five minutes. The rest was forcefully dedicated to the already long evening prep.

'As you all know we are still in progress to commence our co-curricular activities, the members of CPA have decided to construct various clubs for the students to participate in,' Mr Hal continued, standing on the mini dais, trying to get absolute attention from squeaking students.

'Though these various clubs are only expected to commence in about a month's time, the members of CPA have decided to inform about these clubs so as to give you all more time to choose the clubs that best suit you.' Mr Hal paused.

Absolute silence fell over grade 10. Even the laziest Last Benchers and 'We Don't Care What' group members were now listening wholeheartedly to every word that came out from Mr Hal's speaker mouth.

Never before had there been such a head-turning co-curricular-related announcement in Morey's Public School.

'There are six various clubs altogether.' Mr Hal continued to read the announcement note, 'The Dance Club, Arts and Crafts Club, Debate Club, Poetry Club, Public Speaking Club, and last we have the Music Club.'

'Wow!' Allen, who was a fierce debater, exclaimed.

'Not exactly what I had expected,' Rodney said to Jeoff.

Thrill waves passed across the huge hall. Mr Hal's announcements surely did enchant the uninterested mob of grade 10.

'This is a compulsory activity.' Mr Hal continued, as he put down the announcement note on the table, 'Every student of every grade must join one club that interests them the most as these clubs are exclusively created with the intension of identifying, developing, and maximizing every student's hidden talent.'

Mr Joseph Matthew suddenly seemed to have occupied a top position in everyone's list of most appreciated people in MPS.

'And we expect each one of you to showcase your potential will and thrive in your skills by strengthening them to the maximum.'

A faint sound of whispers erupted in clusters across grade 10.

'Dance Club!' Edy and Barrie called out simultaneously. They decided dance was their best cup of tea among the six various clubs.

'No, Debate Club!' Allen interrupted.

'I'm joining Poetry,' Celia said.

'I think I will try Music Club,' Mable said. 'Sounds exhilarating to me.'

Clusters of whispers erupted throughout the class.

'Public Speaking.'

'Music Club sounds great.'

'No, not Arts and Crafts, Jeoff.'

'Who's with me for Debate?'

'Poetry is no better.'

'Dance? I don't think so.'

'How about we suggest a Gardening Club?'

'No, please, hate poetry.'

'Public speaking is dull, Makk.'

'Not changing my choice on Debate Club, Bennett.'

'Fine, go ahead with dance then.'

'Brenda, would you like to join Arts and Crafts with me?'

'Are you kidding me? Music Club? Seriously?'

'I'm done choosing, Debate is final.'

'Jade, no, public speaking is suicidal.'

'I knew you would go for poetry.'

'I don't even know a single dance move.'

'All right, all right,' Mr Hal interrupted the enthusiastic mob. 'You all can discuss and choose your clubs later on, you have got a month's time.' Mr Hal's interruption did not stop the cheerful muttering crowd.

'But make sure you choose the right club, as once you register as a member of a particular club, you possibly cannot shift to another one,' Mr Hal said. 'Now back to computers.' He opened the computer text while the students kept discussing which club they wanted to join.

By one in the afternoon, all the senior grade students were heading to the dining hall, which was huge enough to seat half the population of MPS at a go. The smell of the freshly cut vegetables triggered a pukey sensation as the senior mob entered the dining hall.

'I should have skipped lunch,' Barrie said, looking at the half a dozen varieties of veggies that were cut into thick slices.

'Me too,' Allen said making a facial expression that was a mixture of discomfort, disappointment, and disgust.

'Look at that new guy,' Barrie said, pointing at an adjacent table, 'sneaking radish slices into his sock.'

'Must be his old school tricks,' Edy said miserably, chewing his own share of radish slices.

The members of the Dining Supervisory Panel finally appeared out of nowhere and took several strolls along the lengthy dining hall to make sure everyone ate their share of vegetables.

'Damn, we should have been in grade 12,' Barrie whined.

'Why?' Edy and Allen asked, puzzled. Barrie pointed at the table where grade 12 students were seated. Edy and Allen noticed a frantic senior secretly donating his share of veggies to a helpless junior seated right behind. He had a 'shut up and take it' look on his face as he gave away the veggies to the scared junior from grade 8.

'We have to wait two more years to get to that stage,' Allen pointed out.

That was probably one of the most horrible hidden truths in MPS—well, actually in any boarding school. All the unpleasant and undesirable things were deliberately passed on to the juniors or the newcomers. If anyone resisted the forceful donation, they'd end up delivering two to three lengthy speeches in assembly instead of the standard one speech.

Almost resembles a state penitentiary, doesn't it? Well, you would know better if you grew up in a boarding school or, more unfortunately, in a jail cell.

'Barrie, I have to tell you something' Edy whispered, not wanting anyone else to hear.

'Please don't tell me you hate the veggies,' Barrie whispered back.

'No . . . I mean yes, I hate the veggies but that's not what I was going to tell you.'

'Okay, what's it about?'

After confirming that the others at the table were busy, Edy spoke with a bit of hesitation. 'Of late I have been observing—' Edy started.

'Observing what?' Barrie interrupted as his curiosity shot up.

'If I manage to peep through the numerous blocking heads till the far end—' Edy paused and sneaked a look at the far end.

Going by the curiosity of Edy's voice and its highly secretive tone, Barrie only expected to hear two possible scenes.

Firstly, he expected to hear about a red fire-breathing dragon that was burning away all the uncooked vegetables. Secondly, he expected to hear about a genie squeezing out of a metal lamp to magically banish all the raw veggies.

'If I manage to peep through till the far end,' Edy continued whispering as he put his palm over his mouth, 'I can see the pretty girl that Bonn has been talking to.'

'What?' Barrie thought to himself and quickly recollected thrice what Edy had just said. The thought-processing part of his brain did not take in Edy's words as genuine at first. But after several times of quick recollection, it finally approved the unanticipated words and sent it to the decision-making part of his brain.

'Okay,' Barrie said, still doubting his hearing capabilities and stretching the word *okay* to about three seconds. He only did that when he was either extremely confused or unimaginably surprised.

'What on earth am I supposed to say to that?' Barrie asked, frowning and, at the same time, rapidly blinking his eyelids.

'Er . . . I meant to say . . . I . . . I,' Edy stammered as he instantaneously thought of a defensive sentence, 'I was only trying to make conversation, a random conversation to get our thoughts off these nauseating veggies,' he assured Barrie, smiling weirdly.

Ah, that was a clever one. The best I could think of right now, Edy thought.

'We have a million things to talk about and this is the one you got right now?' Barrie sighed.

'I told you Edy likes the pretty one,' said Allen, who had been eavesdropping on the secretive conversation. His pointy ears were alert enough to have picked up the faint discussion.

'Oh shut up, Allen.' Edy grunted hard. 'That's the last time you are ever gonna say something like that, *ever.*'

Allen smiled before he spoke again, 'Yeah, like that's gonna happen.'

Edy helplessly murmured away while Barrie sat sniggering.

*   *   *   *   *   *

It was the last hour of the day, and Miss Andrella was back with the scored papers as she had promised. Fear filled the atmosphere in grade 10. This was not only the first test on the chapter 'The Kingdom of Kutonians' but also a test on the efficiency and attentiveness of the students. It was the first chance to make a positive impact on Miss Andrella and gain her confidence. It was also the first chance to get into the 'pride spotlight' among the forty-eight pupils. The scores did mean a lot to them, especially to the ones who made each day count. The others who counted to make it through each day didn't really bother.

Miss Andrella stood on the mini dais as the tension grew among the motionless mob.

'These are the final scores of the first test,' said Miss Andrella, shuffling the answer sheets to put the highest scored paper at the end.

I hate this habit of hers or somewhat similar lines were going through most of the old students' minds as they knew the exact method of Miss Andrella's distribution of the valued papers. It was called the mean distribution.

Miss Andrella, unlike other teachers, had the habit of distributing the lowest scored papers first and the highest scored papers last. In this way she could both insult and appreciate the least score and the highest scorer, respectively.

How cruel can she get was what most of the lowest scorers thought. The newcomers, anyhow, had not gotten a change to taste what it was like to score the lowest or the highest in Miss Andrella's paper.

Barrie's sixth sense already sensed that his paper would be among the lowest scored ones, and according to the method of Miss Andrella's mean distribution, he would be among the first few to receive his scored sheets. Sadly he was right about his poor performance when she announced Barrie's name just a few seconds after she had started with the mean distribution. A dozen of the students had horrible scores that shocked even Miss Andrella. The scores were below the baseline, which was 20.

'Ray Anderson, 20 on 50

'Heith, 21 on 50

'Jade, 22 on 50

'Sylvia, 24 on 50

'Daffney, 24 on 50

'Melinda, 24 on 50

'Barrie, 26 on 50

'Eric Reez, 26 on 50

'Craig, 28 on 50

'Ivan Anderson, 29 on 50

'Robin Reeves, 32 on 50

'Jeoff, 32 on 50

'Benn, 32 on 50

'Mable, 34 on 50

'Irennica, 35 on 50

'Joe, 38 on 50

'Morvin, 38 on 50

'Celia, 39 on 50

'Florentina, 39 on 50

'Rodney, 39 on 50

'Santana, 39 on 50

'Makk, 40 on 50

'Swithen, 40 on 50

'Bennett, 41 on 50

'Laana, 41 on 50

'Wenda Alexander, 42 on 50

'Bonn, 42 on 50

'Levangie, 43 on 50

'Allen, 44 on 50

'Reeda, 44 on 50

'Reny, 45 on 50

'Edy, 46 on 50

'Veranna, 47 on 50

'Margretta, 47 on 50'

As the scores kept going up, more students were eager to listen to Miss Andrella. It took not more than three minutes for her to distribute almost all the answer sheets. Well, she did take a lot of time giving scary eye-popping looks to those who scored less than twenty. She also gave broader and broader smiles as the scores went up.

'Damn it! 26 on 50,' Barrie cried.

'Damn it! 46 on 50,' Edy whined.

'Wow! 44 on 50,' Allen exclaimed.

'And the highest scorer of the first test is—' Miss Andrella paused, holding the last answer sheet and with what looked like probably the broadest smile ever. 'Troniya Baikishh,' she proudly announced, '49 on 50.' Loud claps followed.

'Troniya Baikishh?' Edy frowned. 'Who's Troniya Baikishh?' he asked, eager to know who could possibly score a staggering 49 on 50.

As the highest scorer walked onto the dais, Edy's eyes widened. His quick-witted detective eyes didn't take more than a millisecond to recognize the pretty face that had lately become very familiar.

Wait, so that's her name—Troniya, he thought. *And what kind of sorcery is this—49 on 50?*

At once Barrie nudged his companion, who was deeply lost in thought. 'You heard that—49 on 50,' Barrie said.

'Yes, I know, unbelievable,' Edy said, still looking at the highest scorer as she collected her answer sheets from Miss Andrella.

Allen saw the opportunity to drag Edy as a potential victim of his humorous comments. He continuously patted Edy's back and said, 'There, at last you have found someone you can both compete with and compete for.'

Edy precisely knew what Allen had meant by that. He was annoyed with Allen's humorous comments.

'And 49 on 50, goddamn.' Allen spoke as he leapt forward, 'Is that even possible? Never for me.'

'Shut up, Allen,' Celia said. 'Edy will only compete with her, not compete for her.'

'Who knows?' Allen said with a 'Who knows what might happen?' look.

'Let's do a quick review of the answers to the five questions,' Miss Andrella said after she had finished with the mean distribution.

As the remaining thirty minutes of the last hour passed in discussing the most relevant answers, most of which came from the highest scorer, no one had expected the day to get worse any further.

The last bells went off. Miss Andrella stood up with a 'Wait—I haven't finished yet' look on her face.

'The first assignment,' Miss Andrella began, 'which carries twenty points—'

The calmed mob now looked frustrated and it got even worse after her announcement.

'I want you all to submit a poem that explains the theme of the chapter "The Kingdom of Kutonians",' Miss Andrella continued with her bizarre request, 'and submit it in the next English hour.' She seemed to have forgotten the next English hour was the first hour the next day, and she made it sound like there was a week to go.

'The poem that's most relevant and best related to the theme of the chapter will get the highest points,' she said and exited the room.

'Can this day get any worse?' Barrie cried, closing his fists tight and looking at the ceiling.

'Oh yes, it can,' Allen started with his hilarious routine. 'If you don't get the rhyming words right and the chapter's theme into your poem, I'm sure your day will get much worse.'

'Right,' Edy said, 'with you around, I'm pretty sure no single day can get any better.'

Celia punched Allen on his shoulder and said, 'Will you ever stop reminding us of all the annoying things? God.'

'Like the Veggie Thursdays?' Allen said.

'Yes, and now the rhyming words and getting the entire theme of the chapter into the poem.'

'People, relax, it's not all that tricky to write down a few rhyming words,' Edy assured his alarmed group.

'Edy, we all know you're good at poems and that ease doesn't apply to all of us,' said Mable, who kind of boasted Edy's exceptional skill at finding rhyming words.

'Are these kinds of assignments normal at MPS?' Jade, the new addition to the first benchers' group asked.

'No, never have we been asked for a poem as an assignment,' Edy revealed.

'I hate writing poems,' said Jade the newcomer.

'And I hate it when you new guys keep asking stupid questions,' said Allen with a bit of rudeness and showing his annoying smile on his pointy face.

'Don't be so mean to newcomers, Allen,' Celia gently said. 'You know they have to get used to our school's customs and its environment.'

Of course, the newcomers did ask countless silly questions to the older students, and Allen hated answering those questions more than writing poems. He sometimes would get so annoyed that he gave away ridiculously unbelievable answers to the newcomers. His advantage was his years of experience in the school which was also the reason why the newcomers chose to question Allen rather than anyone else.

It was only a week ago when Swithen, a newcomer, had enquired of Allen about the deserted church which was located at the far end of the school premises.

'It's not compulsory to visit the church and not many churchgoers around,' Allen said dejectedly, 'well, except the new ones who also happen to be curious explorers.'

One of the most hilarious of all questions was when Allen overheard Laana, a newcomer probably fond of food, asking Wenda Alexander why they had to eat toasted bread and scrambled egg thrice a week for breakfast.

Almost a hundred questions from the newcomers ran through Allen's extremely sensitive ears.

'Why do we have two school anthems?'

'Why are there so many exotic species of birds around?'

'Was it through fair means or foul tricks that this school won the number one position in the inter-school athletic meet?'

'Why did the previous principal quit? Was it because he was too lenient and the management forced his resignation?'

'Why don't we have horses when there are several stables?'

'Is it true there is a huge water canal running at the rear end of this school?'

'Why don't we have any married couples as teachers?'

'When does the blueberry tree at the end of our corridor bear fruit?'

'Is it true that some students were caught possessing electronic gadgets the previous year?'

'Where exactly is the laundering bay?'

Loads and loads of similar kinds of curious questions came in every day for the first two months. While some enjoyed answering those questions, some including Allen were annoyed even to listen to the newcomers' queries. He finally made up his mind to have fun with the newcomers. This was when he decided to give absurd explanations to the questions.

For example, Allen explained, 'Because the state penitentiary illegally acquired some of the school's property to build jail cells and put notorious criminals next to our school premises,' to the question asked by curious Cyrus, 'Why is the compound wall of this school not exactly rectangular, square or round shaped?'

He also managed to make Jade believe the most preposterous thing when he said, 'Oh, I have personally seen two of them, with my own eyes, especially after twelve at night and mostly around the huge maple tree that you can see when you peep out of the window next to your bed,' to the question 'This place is so full of scary-looking gigantic trees, do you think there are ghosts around here?' Not to mention how quickly Jade had his bed shifted to a more populated corner of the dormitory, far from the window that he had previously been next to.

And he had almost got into trouble with the new boys' warden, Mr Grey Garrison, when the latter heard Allen saying, 'Those two towers were the dumping places for the dead soldiers who were brutally killed in wars many centuries ago,' to the question asked by a junior newcomer, 'What are those two colossal towers for and how long have they been there?'

The latest one to be added to Allen's 'unbelievable explanations to the newcomers' list was the one explanation that sparked a one-hour-long debate on whether angels, specifically protective guardian angels existed or not and if they did, would they ever visit Morey's Public School. This occurred when few students heard Allen saying, 'Oh that noise! That's the noise of the footsteps of the protective guardian angels who only appear at night to protect us from the many invisible intruders,' to the curious question asked by curious Cyrus, 'Of late I have been hearing someone strolling on the sidewalk of our dormitory, around midnight, who could it be?'

'That's an absurd explanation,' curious Cyrus insisted. 'Why would the angels walk when they can fly?'

'Oh, that's because this is a no-fly zone,' Allen said to his confused questioner.

As the boys lined up for their evening games, Barrie had butterflies sitting in his tummy. 'I don't think I'll be joining you guys for the basketball practice today,' he dejectedly said, not wanting to skip games.

'Come on, Barrie, it's just a poem,' Edy tried to pacify his pal. 'Trust me, it's not gonna be so hard to put a few random rhyming words into random sentences.'

Barrie didn't seem to be convinced.

'Moreover, I heard we could use some help from the library,' Jade, the new addition to Edy's group, said. 'Maybe we can copy a few rhyming words and put them in organized sentences.'

'Now why didn't I get that idea?' said Allen.

'By the way, Allen, I wanted to ask you,' Jade started as the group passed by the horse stables.

'Not another one,' Allen sighed as he expected another one of those newcomers' curious questions.

'Why are there no horses when there are stables?'

'The school got rid of them,' Allen answered.

'Why? I love horse riding.'

'Budget cuts,' Allen pointed out. 'The management is trying to trim down expenses.'

'That's awful,' Jade grimly sighed.

*　　*　　*　　*　　*　　*

The clock struck six as the students of MPS rushed back to their respective classes. It was time for the routine two-hour-long prep and all that occupied the minds of grade 10 was one common fear—the poem on 'The Kingdom of Kutonians'.

'What do I do now?' said Barrie with a vexed look. 'I'm so dead.' On his desk was an empty sheet of paper and a refilled blue fountain pen.

'Why don't you start writing down some words relating to kingdom or . . . war or . . . battleground,' Edy suggested.

'And?'

'And see if you can find some rhyming words.'

'What if I don't find any rhyming words?'

'I'm sure you will if you try,' Edy said to cheer his worried companion.

As the hour passed by, Edy took a glimpse of Barrie's paper, which had the exact rhyming words that Celia had in hers. Edy shook his head in dismay.

'What's wrong?' Barrie asked.

'Stop with the photocopying,' Edy said with disenchantment.

'No, I didn't.'

'Yes, you did.'

'No . . . okay, a few words from Celia,' Barrie agreed.

'*Every word*,' Edy sighed.

Barrie put his head down.

'I know it's hard, Barrie, but give it a try, just once,' Edy pleaded.

'Fine, I will,' Barrie said, looking at Edy's written sheet. 'Let me just take a look at yours.'

'But no photocopying, okay?' Edy warned with a grin.

Barrie read though the first few lines of the unfinished poem. 'This is some good stuff,' he said as he continued to read out the rhyming words from Edy's half-done poem, 'knights–fights, strain–vain, rain–pain, tears–years, both–oath, sides–tides, doves–cloves, breed–weed, forget–regret, fields–yields.'

Barrie was astounded. 'Wow, this looks so simple and yet so brilliant, impressive.'

'I'm glad,' Edy said, taking back the poem from his delighted companion.

Immediately, Barrie tore his copied version and started to work on a new one and after much scribbling, scratching, and squiggling, he finally seemed to have found a few rhyming words.

'Edy, how about these?' he asked and read out his own set of original work. 'Kings–wings, flowers–towers, swords–chords, sound–pound, yeast–beast, blood–wood, noose–goose, kill–will.'

'I must admit those are pretty good,' Edy complimented him.

Barrie's ray of enthusiasm glimmered right through his ability to perform at will. 'I can do it!' said Barrie with a lot of zeal filling his voice.

'Yes, you can, Barrie,' Edy said motivationally. 'Now try and put them in a sequential order that reflects the storyline of the chapter.'

'Done,' Barrie said with a burst of vigour. 'And I thought this day couldn't get any better.'

The next morning, all the grade 10 students were geared up with their own unique version of the poem on the chapter 'The Kingdom of Kutonians'. Miss Andrella was flabbergasted to see that not a single student had failed to submit the assignment. She thought the seriousness among the pupils largely came from the fact that they all were in grade 10, the first major turning point in their academic career. The next major turning point was only two years away—grade 12.

'While I go through the poems,' Miss Andrella said after she had collected the forty-eight unique poems, 'I would like you all to brush up on the next chapter, "The Huntsmen of Humberland".'

Nervousness infiltrated the hearts of the lousy poets as they heard another weird request of Miss Andrella. It wasn't about brushing up on the next chapter, 'The Huntsmen of Humberland'.

'I will sort out the best poems, and the respective students will come up on the dais and read these out to the others,' Miss Andrella said and started off with the first poem.

'Do you think my poem will get shortlisted?' Barrie asked sceptically.

'You can stop worrying about it, dear,' a jealous Celia said. 'That's not gonna happen, not with rhymes like "kill–will", "noose–goose", and "flowers–towers".'

Barrie grunted in silence.

Most of the students looked scared and some were very embarrassed, mostly because their rhyming words did not exactly sound like rhyming words and also because the sequence of the chapter was jumbled up.

Though the chapter 'The Huntsmen of Humberland' was what was seen on everyone's desktop, the chapter 'The Kingdom of Kutonians' was what was primarily going through the worried minds.

Barrie and Edy, the first benchers, noticed Miss Andrella's selection of a dozen of poems that included Edy's as well.

'Edy, saw that? She set your paper aside,' Barrie whispered, 'Seems like your poem didn't turn out to be so good after all.'

Miss Andrella had about a dozen of sheets on one end and the rest at the other end of the table.

'I'm surprised how majority of them got the poem right, including me,' Barrie whispered as the sorting process came to an end.

'The ones she set aside on her right are the best ones, you idiot,' Allen quickly reacted.

'Stop calling him that,' Celia said with her right eyebrow hoisted.

'I see someone else got offended too,' Allen said, 'I'm sorry, but you should blame the ineffectiveness of his ability to interpret simple, obvious data.'

'These eight poems are the best among all,' Miss Andrella said as she stood up, holding the shortlisted eight sheets of paper.

The curious crowd got more curious.

'Wenda Alexander,' Miss Andrella announced.

'That mean CR,' Mable grunted, looking at Wenda Alexander as she recalled a handful of the numerous catfights that they had occasionally had over the years at MPS.

Wenda Alexander the secondary class representative went up to the dais to read her version of the poem. She had included some appealing rhyming words which sounded a lot more complicated than any other poem.

Some of them were 'mutilate–speculate, rhythmic–pathetic, wretched–drenched, cruelty–peculiarity, bloody heads–muddy threads, abbreviate–assassinate, pierce–fierce, and elucidate–infuriate'. Of course she did get a loud round of applause for the tricky words that she had used.

The next was Veranna's poem. Her version of it almost literally dramatized the chapter itself, on the mini dais. Some of her rhyming words included 'sins–kin's, slave–grave, decorate–dictate, dead–led, wine–shine, weary–fairy, beggary–smeary, kingly–singly'.

The next five poems more or less sounded similar to each other, except the one by Reeda, which was particularly disturbing as she had deliberately included the blood-shedding and arrow-piercing scenes of the war rather than conveying the message of the chapter. There were many sensitive ones, mostly girls, murmuring 'Eww' at certain intervals, mostly when she described the beheading of prisoners of war (POWs) and the killings of innocent civilians, for which she did not get any applause from the eww-struck mob.

'Next,' Miss Andrella continued, squinting down at the last paper, 'Edy Ravenden.'

Edy very nervously went up onto the dais to read out his unique version of the poem. He was half expecting the crowd to abruptly burst out into loud laughter at his rhyming words. Taking a deep breath and a blind leap of faith, he read out loud.

Neither the Kings nor the Knights
Liable for the Sorrowful Fights,
Raising the Homely Strain,
Earned by the Kings in Vain,
Darkened was the Blood Rain,
Every soul was left in Pain.

Visible was the Myriad of Tears,
Now, having shed them for Many Years,
Hatred fell upon Sides of Both,
Delighted they were when they swore in an Oath,
Still they were no better than Angry Goats.

Hospitable were the People Now,
Of Whom many were filled with Love,
Visible was the Victory on their Sides,
Entertained they were by the High Tides,
Yet, they could Sight the Battle Rides.

Bowing to the Peaceful Doves,
On the high hills of Cloves,
Knight after Knight,
In the Darkness of the Nights,
Sound of them seemed to Regret,
Now, how could they forget?
In the Blood-Red Battle Fields,
Renowned for the number of Death Yields,
Encouraging the Sorrows to Breed,
And the Kutonians have nothing but the Weed.

The Fields would have been Green,
If the Kings were not so Mean,
And a Knight is the one who needs
An affable King who Happily Leads,
Years will Undeniably roll down in Peace.

*   *   *   *   *   *

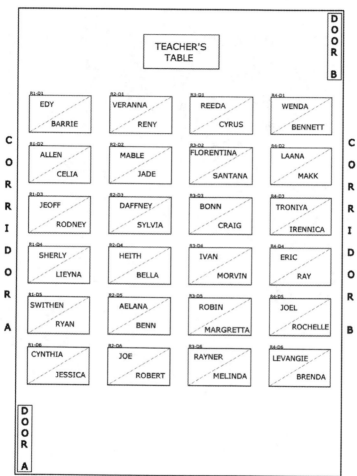

The classroom of grade 10 with all the newcomers.

The Blind Choice

Wednesday, 2 August 2006

August, the dampest month of the year, had more rains to offer than any other month. As the students lined up for their inevitable boring, routine school assembly, the heavens above drizzled millions of cold, foggy miniature drops. Only on the heavy rainy days were the students spared from the 'two school anthems' assembly.

As the first anthem drove to an end, Mr Joseph rushed to give his once-a-week routine speech and all that he could see from behind the podium was the green army of four-hundred-odd students. Their green school sweaters perfectly camouflaged with the greenery of the numerous evergreen trees surrounding the school premises. Adding to the blend was the slow-moving light-ash-coloured cotton-shaped clouds that blinded the most of the sunlight. As the light smoky fog dominated the air, the rays of the golden sun glimmered through the tiny gaps in the marching clouds.

Most of the newcomers did confess that the serenity of the clammy atmosphere did match the heavenly Garden of Eden of the Adam-and-Eve era. Mr Joseph quickly ended his usually lengthy speeches and the choir sang through the second of the two lengthy school anthems. The drizzling intensified and the junior grades' students started to quickly disperse.

'So, how are things going on in grade 10?' the talkative Terry from grade 11, standing adjacent to Barrie, asked.

'Everything's quite as customary as it can possibly get,' Barrie swiftly replied to his friendly senior.

'Yeah, except the increased number of attempts that Bonn is making to try and net a pretty greenhorn,' Allen joined in.

'Is that true?' a shocked Terry asked. 'Another one?'

'Everything I say is true,' Allen cheerfully muttered, 'well, at least when it comes to Bonn.'

'That will add another one to his "failed attempts to net a greenhorn" list,' an informed classmate of Terry, Joey, said. 'Who's that pretty greenhorn, by the way?'

'The one right behind Wenda Alexander,' Edy spontaneously said, looking at the girls' queue at the far left end, 'with the fallen hair and bright look.'

'The one talking to Tina Marvel?' Terry asked, pointing his eyes at the far left end. Allen and Barrie nodded.

'What are you guys talking about?' a doomed Bonn, who coincidentally made his way to the front, entered the unfortunate conversation.

'Just in time, Bonn! What a coincidence!' Terry replied with an evil giggle.

'Why?' Bonn asked, transfixed.

Edy put his arm around Bonn and directed his sight towards the subject of discussion. 'Can you see what we were talking about?' Edy said with a haughty smile.

'I'm sure he can't miss someone that conspicuously elegant,' Barrie said.

Bonn's keen sense of sight sensed an awkward conversation as he saw Troniya among the girly mob. 'Did you guys actually believe what they said about me?' an annoyed Bonn asked.

'Of course, we all did,' Patrick, the class representative of grade 11 who had been eavesdropping, joined the conversation.

'Who wouldn't when you are involved with the pretty greenhorns?' Terry said, trying to control his excited giggle.

'Or should we say an over-involvement?' Edy said and titters of laughter sprang out from the listeners.

'And look, she's looking at us now,' Terry said.

'Probably looking out for Bonn,' Patrick continued as the laughter got louder. 'Why don't you wave at her, Bonn?'

Bonn's face instantly turned pinkish red. The laughter of the students pricked him, humiliated at being the subject of their amusement.

'But why am I getting the feeling that she's looking at Edy and not me?' Bonn whined. Edy turned back at the far left end as thousands of droplets drizzled between the two onlookers.

'Maybe because you're trying to get yourself out of this awkward situation by directing it towards Edy,' Barrie said and his words fuelled the already loud laughter.

'No, I'm serious,' Bonn moaned out. 'Take a look for yourselves.'

'Nice try, Bonn,' Joey said, patting Bonn's back.

As the drizzle intensified, the exposed senior mob put their heads low to avoid their faces from getting wet.

'I hate you guys.' Bonn continued whining as he shook his head in dismay and walked grumpily, 'I have told you like a hundred times she's just a *friend*.'

'I wish we all could believe that, Bonn,' Barrie whispered as they approached the senior class corridor.

'Why doesn't Ivan Anderson get targeted?' Bonn asked, trying to avoid the slippery part of the floor.

'Bonn!' Terry sighed deeply, 'Nobody likes to talk about the most obvious act that Ivan Anderson does in MPS.'

'True that!' Patrick acknowledged and Edy and Barrie nodded in agreement while Bonn's thumping got louder with every step as they raced towards grade 10.

While the students of grade 10 settled down for Miss Andrella to arrive, Edy sat numb, staring at the huge blackboard.

'What's keeping you busy?' Barrie asked.

'I need to tell you something,' Edy whispered in a tone that instantaneously caught Barrie's full attention.

'I'm listening,' Barrie whispered too in a similar tone.

'Not now,' Edy insisted, 'break time.'

'Done,' Barrie agreed, with thumbs-up sign.

What could he possibly have to tell me? Barrie thought hard for the next two hours until finally the class was empty for the coffee break.

'Tell me, what's up?' Barrie fanatically asked.

At first Edy hesitated quite a bit, but he couldn't keep his little secret to himself. He was forced to let it out, especially to Barrie, his best pal.

'Are you gonna tell me or what?' Barrie asked again as he stood up.

'Bonn wasn't trying to escape from being humiliated back at the assembly,' Edy feebly revealed.

'What are you talking about?' Barrie shrugged. 'I don't get it.'

'Well, Bonn wasn't lying after all when he said Troniya was looking at me,' Edy said in a languid manner.

'*She* was looking at *you*?' Barrie asked disbelievingly.

Edy nodded in slow motion and took a cursory glance at Barrie's suspicious expression.

'You are not taking a silly coincidence this seriously, are you?'

'No,' Edy swiftly replied, 'this has been happening for quite a long time.'

'How long are we looking at?' Barrie frowned.

'About three to four weeks.'

'And you didn't care to tell me about it,' Barrie said, his tone turning slightly aggressive.

'I tried to tell you,' Edy insisted.

'When?' Barrie shrugged.

'Dining hall, when I told you I could see her.'

'Dining hall?' Barrie said and paused for a moment to recollect. 'Right, right, I remember,' Barrie said, 'but you just said you could see her.'

'I was gonna tell you more,' Edy sighed, 'but you were—'

'Oh damn, I remember,' Barrie interrupted, and he recollected, 'It was a Thursday.' Barrie continued, feeling sorry for his pal, 'The surprise test, the veggies, all came upon me, I'm so sorry.'

'That's okay,' Edy said. 'Wasn't your fault, it was a Thursday.'

'So that explains why you keep nudging me to move to the right,' Barrie briefly interrupted.

Edy dimly nodded in agreement.

'So tell me, do you think she's attracted to you?' Barrie asked.

Edy forcefully controlled his blushing smile before he said no, with an extended *o*. 'I have a strong feeling it's the other way round.'

Barrie's eyes widened while his eyebrows rose. 'Are *you* attracted to *her*?'

'Um . . . no . . . no . . . maybe,' Edy stuttered. 'I don't know.' He paused with an extended *ow*.

'Maybe you're considering the wrong interpretation,' Barrie said.

'I'm listening,' Edy said inquiringly.

'Maybe she's wondering why you keep looking at her.' Barrie continued explaining his theory, 'And you are wondering why she keeps looking at you.'

Edy kept frowning at Barrie's possible theory.

'That's how everything starts, you see.' Barrie stopped.

'What's everything?' Edy asked, confused.

'Infatuation.'

'What?'

'Infatuation,' Barrie, the self-taught expert on the subject, continued explaining further, 'the state of being carried away by unreasoned passion or, in your case, reasoned admiration.'

'I don't understand,' Edy admitted.

'What's the first thought that comes to you when you think about her?' Barrie asked like an amateur interrogator.

'Well'—Edy briefly paused as his eyes swayed from side to side—'she's exceptionally good at academics.'

'The first test,' Barrie reminded him.

'Yes,' Edy declared, '49 on 50—that's undeniably extraordinary.'

'Just as I had anticipated,' Barrie said, feeling a deep sense of achievement.

'I still don't get it,' Edy glumly admitted.

'Apparently you have a soft spot for the highest scorers,' Barrie started explaining his second theory. 'You like them, the ones who make it to 46, 47, 48, and 49 on 50, irrespective of how close they are to you.'

'No, that's not true,' Edy firmly insisted, 'I don't like Wenda Alexander or Veranna or—'

'I'm referring to the prettier ones,' Barrie said with a 'You know who I am referring to' smile.

'There are no other pretty ones who compete with Wenda or Veranna or . . . or . . . even with me, except—'

'Exactly my point,' Barrie interrupted, with a rather excited voice that echoed through the empty hall. His enthusiasm reached its peaks as he thought he had gotten to the bottom of Edy's mystery affection or, more precisely, attraction.

'Troniya,' Barrie said, placing both his hands on the desk and leaning towards Edy, 'is the only girl you find pretty.' Barrie continued with an increased pitch, 'And she is the only one who could score 49 on 50—that's like two shots from one bullet.'

'That's a rather reasonable explanation,' Edy faintly spoke after a moment of brief thought-filled silence. 'How could you get through this so easily? I thought my mind had been playing tricks all this while.'

'That's what friends do,' Barrie proudly said. 'Only a true friend knows what's going on in his best friend's mind.'

Edy smiled in gratitude as he felt their friendship was only getting stronger with every passing trouble they both managed to get through.

'And I strongly hope your infatuation remains as an infatuation without escalating to limerence,' Barrie hopefully said.

'The what-rence?' Edy asked quizzically.

'Limerence,' Barrie defined, 'an involuntary state of mind which results from a merry attraction to another person combined with an overwhelming, obsessive need to have one's feelings reciprocated.'

Edy stared in panic.

'It's a psychological term,' Barrie added. It didn't make much difference to Edy which branch of science the term was classified into. The meaning was clearly unclear to him as he stared at Barrie with his half-closed eyes.

'Let's just say it's the more serious form of infatuation,' Barrie said.

Edy mentally panicked more. He, though not very deeply, understood what he had gotten himself into.

'I don't understand,' Barrie said with a bemused tone. 'How did this even start in the first place?'

'The poem day.'

'The poem day?'

'Yup,' Edy continued, 'remember we wrote a poem on the Kingdom of Kutonians a few weeks ago?'

Barrie nodded as he constantly bit his thumbnail.

'And I went up to read my version of it.' Edy explained as Barrie keenly listened, still biting his thumbnail.

'And?' Barrie interrupted in excitement.

'As I was reading out the poem, I happened to look at her, several times.'

'And?' Barrie interrupted again. He was more than just excited to listen to Edy's first moment with the pretty newcomer.

'I clearly did notice her smiling at me.' Edy continued, 'Seemingly it wasn't similar to the smile that the rest had nor was it the kind of smile that I had ever seen before . . . I was mesmerized.'

'Prettiattrification smile.' Barrie nodded as he interrupted for the third time.

'The what smile?' asked Edy, somewhat annoyed by Barrie's eerie words.

'Prettiattri—never mind,' Barrie said. 'The definition is not as tricky as the word sounds.'

'Explain,' Edy insisted.

'It's the unconscious brain activity that involves an involuntary, unreasoned pick of an attractive personality or their peculiar expression from a crowd that has exactly the same expression.'

'You know how much I hate it when your explanation gets as vague as it can get,' Edy whined.

'Let me explain with an example.' Barrie continued as he sat on top of the desk, 'Picture this, there are a hundred people looking at you, all having the exact same expression or, in your case, the smiling expression.'

'Okay,' Edy said with an extended *kay* as he started to visualize the poem-reading scene.

'At first you don't see the slightest difference in their appearances, but as you scan the crowd, your brain, without your consent, picks up one face/smile from the hundred-odd faces or smiles, the same face or smile which you think is out of ordinary—that one smile called the prettiattrification smile.'

Edy recollected the out-of-the-ordinary smile that his brain had picked up from the group of smiles.

'*Pretti* is the short form for pretty person. *Attri* is the short form for attraction and so a pretty face that has an attractive smile is called the prettiattrification smile— that's the one your brain unconsciously picked up,' Barrie explained.

'And why exactly did my brain pick up the out-of-the-ordinary, prettiattri-something smile?' Edy questioned.

'Back to square one,' Barrie swiftly answered with a cheerful smile, 'infatuation.'

'So it's an endless loop that would eventually lead to a disaster?' Edy asked.

'Yes,' Barrie confirmed, 'disaster only if you can't get your feelings reciprocated.'

Oh God! Edy thought.

'How did you become such an expert on this subject?' Edy curiously asked.

'Forgot about my dad's profession, didn't you?' Barrie asked.

'Oh right, right,' Edy said delightedly, 'how could I forget your dad, a renowned psychiatrist?'

'Prettiattrification is the new thesis that he's working on,' Barrie said.

Both Edy and Barrie were lost in thoughts, recollecting what the other had said. Both had one thought as they rewound what the other had just explained—*How astounding! I don't know if I should take his words seriously, but it seems interesting.*

'Poor Bonn.' Barrie finally broke the silence. 'Just a few hours ago, I was under the false impression that he was the one trying to get away from the awkward situation.' He continued with a smug smile, 'Now it's clear that you are the one who was escaping from it.'

'You know how much I hate being in the spotlight and gaining unnecessary attention,' Edy sighed.

'And I, being your best friend, don't even get a clue on what you are up to,' Barrie complained. 'You are always so hesitant when it comes to sharing your secrets.'

'That's because you hate keeping secrets.'

'No, I don't.'

'You hate keeping them from Celia.'

'Yes, I do.'

'That's why I'm so hesitant,' Edy whined. 'Boys' secrets should remain with the boys.'

'I just told her one big secret.'

'The "cat ate the bird" secret?'

'No, the "Bryan was beaten in bathroom" secret.'

'You told her that?' Edy moaned in disappointment.

'Yes,' Barrie energetically said, 'that was undeniably an epic one among all the fights that have happened in MPS.' Barrie continued while Edy put his hands over his head, 'All your strong blows on Bryan's face, all the nosebleeds he had, and the "fell on slippery floor" lie that he told the medical intern at the school hospital.'

Edy clenched his teeth and stared irately at Barrie.

'Oh, by the way,' Barrie revealed, 'I also told Celia the "cat ate the bird" secret.'

'Oh God!' Edy exclaimed while Barrie kept going.

'She did feel a little sad for the bird though.'

'Argh!' Edy grunted in disappointment.

'What's next?' Barrie asked after a brief thought-filled moment.

'I don't know, what do you propose I do next?'

'Try and talk to her, befriend her,' Barrie proposed, which Edy didn't appreciate as he knew it was easier said than done.

'No way, not when there are so many curious people are around,' Edy defied him.

'Then there's no possible way to get going on that,' Barrie pointed out.

The recess bells went off. Grade 10 was back to life with swarming students back in class. In no time, Mr Hal entered grade 10 and stood on the mini cemented dais, looking happier than usual.

Must be another announcement from the Chambers of Principal Authority, everyone thought. They were half right and half wrong. It was the announcement from the CPA but not a new one.

'As you all know, the members of CPA had created various clubs for the students to participate in.' Mr Hal's words began to instantly grab everyone's attention. 'I am here today to announce that the six various clubs will commence operations starting from next Saturday, 12 August.'

All the gossip vanished in the blink of an eye and the Last Benchers sat erect to have a clear view of Mr Hal.

'Every Saturday, from 1 p.m. to 4 p.m., all the students will remain at their respective clubs and participate in the various events.' Mr Hal continued enchanting the students, 'That's three hours every week dedicated exclusively for co-curricular activities.'

Mr Hal's announcement became all the more interesting with every word he spoke. 'I will now announce the names of the six various clubs,' Mr Hal said, opening his thick, paper-filled brown cardboard file. 'Those who are interested, please raise your hands while I note down your names under the respective club's register.'

The students of grade 10 turned impatient. Some had still not chosen their best suited clubs. Many were convincing their stubborn friends to join a particular club, and yet some were only adding more confusion for no particular reason, mostly the nonsense ones of the class.

As Mr Hal opened the register of the first club, something clever seemed to have struck Edy's perspicacious mind as he thought of a plan.

The blind choice, Edy thought, and his proud smile dominated his enlightened face.

'First we have the Arts and Crafts Club,' Mr Hal announced, uncapping his school-sponsored pen. A good deal of hands went up in the air amid the chaos. As far as the class was concerned, the Arts and Crafts Club was the most easy-going among all the clubs. The prospective members of this club would only be expected to showcase different types of paintings, art, and craft works that were as colourful as the decorated Christmas tree.

Edy deliberately looked back to see if Troniya had raised her hand for the Arts and Crafts Club. *Right, why would she go for the easy one? She's not that incompetent*, he thought as he took a glimpse at row 4, desk 3.

'We're fixed on the Dance Club, right?' Barrie asked desperately, waiting for Mr Hal to announce the next club.

'Maybe,' Edy said. Mr Hal quickly noted down the names for the Arts and Crafts Club.

'What do you mean, "Maybe"?' Barrie frantically spoke, 'I thought we decided on this one a month ago.'

'We . . . we . . . had . . .' Edy stammered, 'but I was thinking . . . just for a change—'

'Well, think fast then,' Barrie anxiously said.

'Next we have the Dance Club,' Mr Hal announced. Edy desperately waited to see if Troniya had raised her hand. Nothing happened at row 4, desk 3.

'Have you decided yet?' an annoyed Barrie asked as he saw Mr Hal noting down the names for the Dance Club. 'Can we join the dance club, please?' Barrie begged.

'No,' Edy replied, 'definitely not Dance Club, let's do something different.' Barrie grunted in disappointment.

'Next we have the Debate Club,' Mr Hal announced soon after jotting down the names for Dance Club.

No, please, not this one! Edy said as faintly as possible. He only expected Troniya to hear his faint words and follow accordingly. There were two reasons why he hated Debate Club. One was because he was not very good at confronting the opponent only with the use of words. That was something far too difficult for him. It always took him more than just words to confront his opponent, the other tool usually being his fists that delivered strong blows on the face. The second reason was the thought that he had to face Allen in the debate. Nothing could possibly get more embarrassing than being a victim of his humorous comments, especially in front of a large crowd that had students from all other grades.

Fortunately for Edy, Troniya did not respond to Mr Hal's announcement.

'Next we have Poetry,' Mr Hal announced.

'I swear to God, I'll kill you if force me into poetry,' Barrie at once warned with a stern look.

A number of girly hands went up, including those of Wenda Alexander and Reeda. This did express their 'deep thinker' character.

Who would want to write poems on a spring evening under a may tree while lovebirds high above dropped mayflowers on the poet? Edy thought even though he was reasonably good at it.

Edy's luck was vibrant enough as Troniya did not respond at all. The only two clubs that remained now were Public Speaking and Music Club—one highly risky and the other moderately risky, respectively.

Edy had butterflies fluttering in his tummy as he took a cursory glance at Troniya when Mr Hal announced about the Debate Club.

Who would want to speak in public, like those greed-driven politicians who keep chattering through giant black speakers on a hot afternoon, boasting about their own achievements and the deeds that they have done for the general public? Edy amusedly thought, *The more desperate ones even launch attacks on the opposition parties.*

Yet there were some assiduous hands that went up in the air when Mr Hal announced the Public Speaking club.

'Thank goodness!' Barrie exclaimed in relief, 'I thought you were gonna join the public speaking club.'

'Nah, who would want to join such a tedious club?' said Edy.

'I still didn't get a reasonable excuse as to why you ditched the pre-decided Dance Club.'

'You will, Barrie,' Edy assured as he turned back at row 4, desk 3.

'Also, I don't understand why you are so concerned about the other,' Barrie said, as he had been observing Edy's anomalous behaviour. 'Why do you keep looking back whenever Mr Hal announces—?'

'Right, Music Club,' Edy said and raised his hand as Mr Hal lackadaisically announced, 'Last we have the Music Club.'

Barrie followed. 'Are you even listening to me?' Barrie whined, 'Who were you looking at all this while?'

Barrie turned back quickly and as he saw what he saw, he exclaimed, 'The blind choice!' At that instant, Barrie realized Edy's intention of ditching the Dance Club and the reason behind joining the Music Club.

'You should have told me,' Barrie complained half-heartedly.

'Wouldn't you have opposed it?'

'I certainly would have,' Barrie admitted, 'I so wanted to join the Dance Club.'

'Good, I just saved us both a lot of time that would have gone wasted in pointless argument,' Edy said with his proud smile back on.

'You,' Barrie said with a rough tone, 'you are one mean guy.' Barrie continued to confront his best friend, 'Clever, too clever to be in Morey's Public School, let alone in grade 10.' Barrie continued, both praising and criticizing his best pal at the same time, 'You always look for two shots from a single bullet.'

'Please don't let me do this all by myself, Barrie,' Edy said in a gloomy tone that added a bit of sentiment to the statement, 'You know I can't do this alone.'

'You bet,' Barrie said. 'What's the point of all this, why did you implement the blind choice in the first place?'

'Creating a common bridge,' pointed out Edy, murmuring his little secretive plan.

'For what good purpose?'

'Cutting down the onlooking curious pairs of eyes from an awful forty-six to a merry seven.'

'Potential pairs of curious eyes,' Barrie corrected in a low voice, 'and for God's sake, Edy, she's our classmate, you can talk to her right here, in our class.'

'Are you nuts?' Edy whined, 'Do you know how much attention that would grab, especially from guys like Allen, Ivan, and Bonn?'

'Great! You are so concerned about their opinion rather than your own,' Barrie murmured.

'I haven't spoken to her once,' Edy admitted. 'And all of a sudden you expect me to go talk to her, what an awkward situation that would be.'

'The situation would only get all the more awkward if she steps forward to talk to you,' Barrie grinned.

'I know, I hope that doesn't happen,' Edy prayed.

'I only want to see one thing when she talks to you,' Barrie cheerfully muttered.

'The overwhelmed look on my face?' Edy asked inquiringly.

'No, a disastrous gloomy-dead look on Ivan Anderson's face,' Barrie said with an evil grin.

'Ivan Anderson? Did I just hear Ivan Anderson's name?' Allen interrupted as he overheard Barrie's excited loud voice.

'No, it was Avon Harrison,' Edy quickly lied with a cover story already hatched in his quick-witted mind. 'We were talking about Avon Harrison, the head of the Chambers of Healthy Dietary.'

'Why would you talk about Avon Harrison?' Allen asked suspiciously.

'We . . . we are hatching a plan to kidnap and threaten him to withdraw his decision to include the veggies on Thursdays,' Edy secretively nudged Barrie as he finished his made-up cover story.

'Yes, yes,' Barrie joined in, 'that's right.'

For five seconds Allen looked at them doubtfully. But it was a cleverly plotted cover story. Even a smart person like Allen had to give in to a well-plotted story like this as it seemed justifiable.

'That's a great idea,' he finally said. 'Don't you guys dare to forget to include me in the plan.'

Edy and Barrie quickly showed the thumbs-up sign in assurance.

Saturday, 12 August 2006

Saturday, 12 August, was the first day for the commencement of the new co-curricular activities—the six various clubs. The students had an uncanny excitement on their faces. You could tell just by looking at the speed at which they marched from the dining hall to their respective clubs that were scattered across the vastness of Morey's Public s School.

As grade 10 split apart into much smaller groups, Edy and Barrie formed a group including five others along with Troniya and Mable and headed towards the Music Club.

As the tiny group entered the Music Club, a group of about forty students from different grades were already taking a self-tour across the huge hall.

Edy's eyes fell upon the well-arranged, brand-new, shining musical instruments that were elegantly arranged in rows and columns. There were several aisles, each one exclusively dedicated for a particular instrument.

'Looks like the management has eased some budget cuts after all,' Barrie said as he stood among the forty-odd members of the Music Club.

As Edy and Barrie walked between the musical aisles, they joined the awestruck students, who were in for a musical treat. They couldn't believe what they were witnessing as the huge hall resembled the abode of the god of music.

There was a pair of classy grand pianos that were double coated with reflective black paint, half a dozen electronic keyboards that were of black and silver, a dozen glossy wax-coated cellos, fancy electric guitars, high-end acoustic guitars, varnished classical guitars and an ornamented eight-stringed guitar, several polished swanky wooden violins.

There was a lonely standing lovely xylophone, several shimmering bugles and beautiful basset horns, shiny metal drum kits, silvery trumpets, showy wooden carved flutes, radiant carved metal harmoniums, several pairs of bongo drums, brand-new synthesizers, plushy wooden harps, a pair of gleaming golden saxophones, and a few flashy flumpets.

'And I was under the impression that nothing could beat Dance Club,' Barrie said as he stared far ahead the aisle crammed with other shrill-noised metal instruments.

'Goddamn,' Edy exclaimed, smoothly running his fingers along the cold flashy flumpets, 'Did the management win a million bucks lottery?'

As the brief awestruck self-tour came to an end, all the new members of Music Club gathered around the desk of the Mr Coogy Cal aka Violin Expert Only. This was the name given to him by the students of MPS. Why? Because he was a violin expert only. He taught no other instrument except violin. The moment the students took a closer look at the violin-only expert, their excitement dropped to the floor.

To add to the disappointment was his unkempt physical appearance. He had the palest face of all pale faces in pale town. His shoes, probably a decade old, were unpolished, his trousers unironed, with tawdry shirt, straggly hair, unshaven face, and sluggish eyes. It seemed like someone paid him a ton to dress up so grubbily. His untidiness was that unnatural.

'If that is how people who are familiar with violin dress up, then I will by all means stop Celia from learning violin,' Barrie murmured, standing at the corner.

'Hello, everyone,' the violin-only expert said, without the slightest sign of enthusiasm on his pessimistic face. 'First of all, I welcome you to the Music Club.' He paused.

The new members stood still for several seconds. Nothing happened for another fifteen seconds.

'Did someone say "Freeze"?' Barrie whispered faintly.

'Shh,' Edy shooed.

'You can choose any one instrument you wish to learn,' he said after an awkward twenty seconds of silence. 'Well, actually two instruments if you would like,' he said, looking into the rule book that was on his glass-topped desk. 'I only teach violin,' he added, 'absolutely no other instrument but violin.'

'Was he lost on an island filled with heaps of violins?' Barrie mockingly asked.

'Maybe,' Edy answered as he minutely observed Mr Coogy Cal's untidy, unironed clothes.

'But not to worry, the management will soon hire a new music teacher to help with the other instruments as well,' he assured the members. About thirty-five of them heaved a sigh of relief. A large part of the group thought everyone would be forced to learn only violin because the pale-faced man was a violin expert only.

'How frustrating it would be to have so many exquisite music instruments lying around and you are forced to learn only violin,' Barrie said to his companion.

'Well, not that frustrating if you actually want to learn violin, it's undeniably one of the melodious instruments on this planet,' Edy said.

'I am considering of replacing the number 1 position in my most hated things in MPS, from Thursday's veggies to this unkempt man,' Barrie whispered again as the violinist tried to gather some more words from his slow brain.

'Now, all those who are interested to learn violin, please raise your hands,' Mr Violinist said taking out the violin register. What happened next only disenchanted Edy.

No! You must be kidding me! Edy thought as he saw what he saw.

Why not? Edy convinced himself as he raised his hand to about his chest level, when he was deliberately stopped and his hand forcefully pulled back to its original position.

'Are you in your senses?' Barrie cried, still holding Edy's struggling hand. 'You really want to be the only guy to join Violin Club?'

'I'm just narrowing it down further,' pointed out Edy.

'Well, I believe you are overdoing it.' Barrie pointed out, 'This would only make your plans so obvious to the others.'

Edy's fighting arm instantly turned lifeless.

'And look, there's Mable,' Barrie's eyes pointed towards Mable's raised hand.

'You're right!' Edy said, feeling grateful.

'And what would Allen say when he hears about this?' Barrie said.

'I forgot he even existed,' Edy said.

'My goodness! Your thoughts are getting carried away so much that you're forgetting the "one bullet, two shots" rule,' Barrie whined. 'Now it's more like "two bullets, no shot".'

Of course Barrie was exceptionally right in his 'two bullets, no shot' theory. The two bullets referred to Edy (a) implementing the clever 'blind choice' plan and (b) successfully cutting down the curious onlookers from forty-eight to a mere five. The 'no shot' referred to the possible leakage of Edy's secret plans to approach Troniya. It took Edy only seconds to realize how Barrie had just saved him from taking a potential bad step.

'Then what do you suggest?' Edy asked, feeling deeply gratified.

Barrie quickly scanned the huge hall filled with glittering and shimmering instruments. His eyes seemed to have gotten attracted to the trendiest instrument. 'Guitar,' he finally decided.

'Guitar?' Edy doubtfully asked.

Barrie frowned before he said, 'Okay, how about xylophone . . . or . . . or . . . flumpet . . . or harp, you choose.'

'Let's just stick to guitars,' Edy said with a cheerful grin on his joy-filled face.

*   *   *   *   *   *

The Meeting That Wasn't

Friday, 8 September 2006

Almost a month had passed by. Everything at MPS was as orderly as usual except for the commencement of the six new clubs. Luckily the school's management had finally found and recruited an additional music teacher who taught many instruments, unlike the pale-faced violinist.

When Mr Michael Raphael was introduced to the students, especially to the members of the music club, they had one obvious thought loitering in their minds—*Why do we need the pale-faced violinist who only taught violin when the management has recruited Mr Michael Raphael, who can teach several instruments?*

It was a funny dilemma when Mr Michael Raphael revealed his defect. As crazy as it sounded, and many called it a one-in-a-million coincidence, Mr Michael Raphael, the new music teacher, was an expert in several instruments but one—the violin. He honestly admitted he was not even a beginner.

The only person who was more than happy to hear about Mr Michael Raphael's shortcoming was the pale-faced violinist. It was only because of the former's limitation that the violinist's job at MPS was saved.

'That's a very lucky recruitment,' Edy said as he heard about the funny dilemma.

'Either that or both the music teachers have had some sort of illegal deal before Mr Raphael was recruited.' Barrie continued as he noticed how short Mr Raphael was, 'I wonder where the management fished this little man from.'

It was, fortunately, Edy's thought that was true—a lucky twist of fate.

Mr Michael Raphael was tidy, clean-shaven, and had his long hair neatly combed. What was more conspicuous about him was the blast of energy on his face unlike the pale-faced violinist. Most could tell that just by looking at him—well, they had to bend a little if they exceeded five feet four inches, to get a face-to-face view of Mr Raphael.

His skills were unobtrusive until he had finally gotten his hands on the musical instruments. His expertise in guitars, keyboards, and drums was all the more intriguing. Like a preprogrammed robot, he showcased all his talent as he fiddled and meddled with all the instruments that he was aware of.

The members of the music club literally had goose bumps when they heard Mr Raphael playing a myriad of familiar tunes. His little round-tipped, skilled fingers moved along the frets of the acoustic guitar like they had been magically detached from his body. The other hand strummed the six shimmering strings to form a melodious rhythm.

'How does he do that?' someone murmured from the enthralled group.

Mr Raphael further impressed the already impressed members of the music club when he effortlessly played through the famous guitar solo, 'Archery-Pan-Stone'.

'I don't know about the violinist, but this guy was surely lost on an island filled with heaps of guitars,' Edy said as Mr Raphael shifted to rock music on the electric guitar.

'Also on an island filled with heaps of other musical instruments,' Barrie said, referring to the other skills of Mr Raphael.

'Except violins,' Edy corrected.

'Right,' Barrie said with a deep giggle, 'all the Violins washed ashore on the island where our pale-faced violinist was stranded.' Edy giggled along with his best pal.

The musical showcase continued for another fifteen minutes and it also continued to inspire the now interested mob to pick up their favourite instruments and kick-start the practice.

Edy had finally gotten a chance to try and talk to Troniya, at least when there were not as many as forty-six pairs of curious eyes all around him and definitely no Allen or Ivan Anderson. His privacy meant a lot to him; so did his hatred of being in the spotlight for dire reasons.

The first hurdle came when the pale-faced violinist got a separate compartment for the six violin learners. He did not mingle with the other members of the music club; neither did his pupils. The six members, all girls, were confined to the violin section and the only person to supervise them was their teacher. Everyone knew how much the violinist hated the loud thuds and thunders of the drum kits, when they saw him with stuffed round cotton balls in his ears. He also hated crowds exceeding a merry ten people. He certainly did look like a complete loser, to Edy at least, as he could not think of any possible route to mingle with the violin learners, especially Troniya.

Providentially for Edy, all the forty members of the music club, irrespective of which instrument they chose to learn, were brought together for the basics. It was Mr Michael Raphael's decision. According to him the basics of music were a must for every member of the music club. It was more of theory rather than practical knowledge. The basics of music included the different types of musical instruments, their origins and history, their significance and roles in the past as well as present, the differentiation between similar kinds of instruments like trumpet and flumpet or drum kits and bongo drums or the grand piano and the electric keyboard. The basics also included the identifying the pitches, notes, and chords that are used to play different instruments.

Of course, majority of the explanation came from Mr Raphael and the remaining small part, mostly the violin basics, came from the violinist. It was decided that one hour was to be dedicated to the basics of music till the 30 September—that was three Saturdays and three hours of basics left for Edy to plan his way of approach.

Great! I have got three weeks to plan, Edy gaily thought, *three Saturdays and three hours to execute them!*

After three days of intense thinking, Edy finally prepared a rough draft of his approach plan. Though the plan was very simple and straightforward, it didn't seem foolproof. The first step of the plan was to shift his seat next to Troniya's, which was easier said than done. The second step was the opening line, famously known as the approach line or, more familiarly, the opening statement.

Edy had written down ten possible opening statements, and when he was not sure which one was the best among those, he finally approached Barrie—the self-taught expert on the subject. To make sure everything was done secretly, they both agreed to decide on the best opening statement when the class was empty. The ten-minute coffee break was their ideal time.

Barrie read through the rough draft of ten opening statements that Edy had prepared and gave his own opinion on each of them.

1) *Hey! I have seen you in my class. You are from Grade 10, right?*—Lame, there are just forty-eight students in our class. She might think you suffer from memory loss.

2) *Hi! I'm Edy! And you?*—Realistic, you could go with this.

3) *I hope Mr Coogy Cal's teaching isn't as bad as he looks*—Unpleasant, giving out negative comments about others might send out a bad impression, plus the violinist is her teacher.

4) *How you doing today? Troniya, right?*—Acceptable

5) *Violin? Why didn't you choose some other instrument?*—Catastrophic, the statement is very authoritative. She loves what she loves.

6) *I have been waiting to talk to you for a while now!*—Creepy, she might as well think you are a lunatic.

7) *Can we meet up somewhere else? I have something important for you*—Suspicious, she would sense something fishy going on.

8) *You know something that you already know about you? You are very, very pretty*—Flirty, she will put you among those whom she considers as pervs.

9) *Would you mind if I sit here? Or are you expecting someone?*—Reasonable, like a gentleman's approach.

As soon as Barrie read through the last opening statement, he burst out into loud laughter. For the next ninety seconds he laughed his lungs out, no matter what Edy did. The unexpected loud laughter swayed his whole body and for a moment threatened to imbalance him.

'Barrie,' Edy shouted as curtly as he could, 'would you stop it now?'

Barrie deliberately controlled his laughter, which did not completely vanish from his lungs. 'Seriously, this is your opening statement?' Barrie asked, still feeling the after-effects of his balance-threatening laughter.

Edy stated in defence, 'I was not intending to use it.'

'Well, if you do, don't forget to take a bouquet of red roses and a diamond ring,' Barrie said, his lungs expelling out the remaining bits of laughter.

'Barrie, please,' Edy sighed. 'That's why I asked you. You are the expert in these matters, not me.'

'Even an expert like Ivan Anderson wouldn't have thought of using such a serious opening statement,' Barrie said with a husky giggle.

'So which one do you recommend?' Edy asked.

'Option 2, 4, or 9, you choose,' Barrie said.

The following Saturday, Edy was half prepared to go ahead with the plan, still not sure which option to choose. As the members of the music club entered the huge hall, he hesitated to implement his very first step—to occupy the seat next to that of Troniya. The room quickly filled up, and Mable and Troniya were seated at the last row. The seats next to them were not yet occupied, and Edy's nervousness had already set in. After a minute of discussion which resembled an argument, with lots of 'No, you go first, I'll follow you', Barrie promptly stepped ahead and occupied the seat that, according to the plan, was supposed to be occupied by Edy.

The minute of argument-like discussion also incorporated a change of plan, which mostly came from Edy who was tremendously jumpy to occupy the empty seat next to Troniya's. The last row was occupied by the seniors, starting from Mable on the extreme left, then Troniya, then Barrie, and then Edy and three empty seats. The right corner was occupied by grade 11 and grade 12 students. The major boost to their start was Mable occupying the corner seat. Had it been occupied by Troniya, the whole plan would have been an utter flop.

Mr Raphael began his lecture on the basics of music while the pale-faced violinist stood at the end of the class. According to the change of plan, Barrie was supposed to switch seats with Edy. As the lecture continued, Barrie thought of a reason to switch seats. Even sitting a scat apart from Troniya, Edy began to notice the changes in his breathing. His heart began to pound harder; his pulse rapidly increased, shortening the intervals between the pulses.

'Edy,' Barrie began, trying to sound as unsuspicious as he could, 'would you like to switch seats? I'm not tall enough to see Mr Raphael from here.'

That was not what he wanted to say. All he really wanted to say was 'Mr Raphael is not tall enough to be seen from this seat.' But that would be dumb. Edy, who was about the same height, would not be able to see Mr Raphael as well. So acting as though he was much shorter than his pal, Barrie decided to go with the first reason.

'Ah . . . er . . . I . . .' Edy mumbled, feeling very nervous to switch seats.

Barrie sternly gave a 'Get up, will you?' look. His serious expression did not seem to overtake Edy's adamant jumpiness.

God, Edy, what's wrong with you? Barrie thought and changed his look to a 'Get up at this instant' expression.

Edy's nervousness was stuck to him like he was stuck to his chair.

Okay, this isn't working, Barrie thought and swiftly stood up.

Barrie's rough action did not seem to catch any attention from the two girls as they continued to listen to Mr Raphael's lecture.

Edy couldn't think of a counteraction plan. At once he switched over and sat right next to Troniya. The new seating arrangement was Mable–Troniya–Edy–Barrie.

The seating was precisely according to the plan, but the impetuous emotions that set in on Edy weren't. He hadn't had a clue as to how speedily his anxiety could churn up right from his spine and spread so evenly all over his body.

For the next fifty minutes, Edy's bodily functions stood at these numbers:

Body temperature: 101.6 degrees Fahrenheit

Pulse rate: 96–106/min.

Blood pressure: 160–179 systolic

Respiratory rate: 25–30/min.

Sweat glands performance at 79 per cent

Thought processing rate: 40–45/min.

Valid thoughts processed: 2 per cent

Invalid thoughts processed: 98 per cent

Decision-making capability: 7 per cent of total capacity

Tension: 72 per cent of total capacity

Uneasiness: 60 per cent of total capacity

Nervousness: 86 per cent of total capacity

Overall conclusion: Patient suffering from sudden exposure to someone/something very acutely desirable/attractive/gorgeous.

What's happening to me? Edy kept thinking to himself as his body changed its course of normality. He took a cursory glimpse at his watch—*1.10 p.m.* He thought, *I have still got fifty minutes.*

He took several deep breaths to try and ward off the mysterious nervous, excited, uneasiness-filled feeling that had been bothering him ever since he sat next to Troniya. Nothing of that sort happened. It only got worse with every passing minute while Barrie got restless after much nudging and signalling his pal to implement step 2— the opening statement.

At 1.20 p.m. sharp, I'll make my move, Edy conclusively said to himself.

1.19 p.m.

Edy's palms turned colder and sweatier at the same time, defying the normal biological characteristic of sweat, which appeared only when there was intense heat. The butterfly effect filled his tummy. He could feel every bit of the miniature shivers that erupted from the inside of his guts. The tension was only shown on his pen as he pressed it hard against the blank sheet. He had a web of thoughts that had become greatly entangled.

I will, I will, I will, he kept repeating over and over.

1.20 p.m.

Okay, I have got a minute . . . sixty seconds is a lot of time, he said to himself, keeping an eye on the second hand of his watch.

55, 54, 53, 52, 51, 50, 49, 48, 47, 46, 45, 44, 43, 42, 41, 40, 39, 38, 37, 36, 35, 34, 33, 32, 31, 30

Thirty seconds, he nervously thought, *nothing to worry about—thirty seconds is half of 'a lot of time' and is also a lot of time.*

Barrie nudged his panicking pal, signalling to make the next move.

I will, Edy signalled with his nervousness-filled eyes.

Time's flying, Barrie gestured with his own set of signals.

1.21 p.m.

Damn Barrie, Edy thought, blaming him for distracting him from keeping his time count.

At 1.30 p.m., I'm not gonna miss, he decided.

Barrie signalled Edy to look into his book.

Are you gonna talk or what? Edy read.

Of course, I will, Edy wrote on the last page of his book.

When? Barrie wrote in reply.

At 1.30, Edy wrote and nodded vaguely.

At 1.30? We didn't exactly plan to launch a rocket, did we? Barrie wrote then drew an angry face at the end of the sentence.

Okay, I will talk, okay?

Do it now, and which option are you going with?

Option 9

Option 9?

Yes. 'Would you mind if I sit here? Or are you expecting someone?' Remember?

You were supposed to say that in the beginning, even before the lecture started, Barrie wrote and drew a second face with a disappointed appearance.

Oh please! We're not enacting Shakespeare's Julius Caesar play now, are we?

Barrie shut his book hard and sat numbly, trying to look like he didn't care anymore.

Edy quickly decided he would go with option 4—*How you doing today? Troniya, right?*—and took another glance at his watch.

It's 1.39 p.m.? What the hell? Edy was alarmed by the rate at which the time was flying. *Is my watch playing some kind of practical joke?*

He made sure it wasn't after he peeked at his neighbour's watch—the one on the right, not on the left.

At 1.50 p.m., not missing on this, I swear, he strongly decided.

Mr Raphael continued the lecture while Mr Violin-Only Expert stood at the other corner.

For the next ten minutes, Edy kept thinking of all the possible situations his move could lead to and the possible replies he could get from Troniya, if any. Most of them turned out to be negative or embarrassing replies.

How would she react? What if she doesn't react at all? I'll look like an idiot, he restlessly thought.

Hell, come what may, you are gonna talk to her, his inner voice cheered him.

What if Mr Raphael notices me talking and asks me to leave? Damn! That would be so embarrassing!

Don't care, at 1.50 p.m., you will go ahead with option 4, his inner voice commanded him.

What if Mable doubts me, she might suspect I'm onto something.

No, Troniya is your classmate, why would Mable get suspicious at all? The confidence-implanting inner voice whined within.

He took another peek at his watch. *1.49 p.m.? Time, why did you have to be so rough on me?* Edy cried to himself.

What's my first move? he asked himself and gave it serious thought as though he was facing a threatening tiger.

I'll turn, smile then talk—no, talk then smile—no, no . . . He realized he had only fifteen seconds to decide on his move. His breaths became shorter and palms drenched in sweat.

Turn and talk and smile or smile and talk and turn, turn smile talk smile, smile talk turn talk, turn smile turn talk, talk smile talk turn—damn!

1.50 p.m.

Talk, talk, talk! Edy's inner voice finally screamed loud in his chest and made him quiver for a quick jiffy. He was in a reluctant battle with his inner voice, vigorously trying to suppress its volume as much as he could.

She's just a girl, Edy, talk to her, for goodness sake, his inner voice screamed at him yet again.

You're not gonna do it, Barrie wrote and nudged Edy to read.

I will, Edy wrote in reply rather tetchily.

You bet?

100 bucks

1000 bucks

Okay, let's not bet on this.

You have got five minutes left, Barrie reminded.

I know, Edy wrote and shut his book again.

Wait, how about I talk to her when the class disperses? In that way, my move won't be as suspicious, Edy thought and waited for the lecture to end.

At 2.06 p.m., Mr Raphael ended his Basics of Music lecture, after which he instructed the class to go ahead with the practical exercise.

Edy again got his intense holding-back feeling that had visited him every time he tried to make his move.

The members started to disperse to their respective sub-clubs; so did Troniya.

'I would have won the bet,' Barrie dimly whispered.

The best Edy could do was to turn to his left and watch her walk away. He tried to take control of his vocal cords and speak out, which did not happen.

'Not a word,' Barrie whined deeply while Edy sat, forcing down the nib of his pen through the empty book. 'Not even a single word.'

'Argh,' Edy grunted to himself and punched his thigh in frustration.

'But don't worry. We've got two more hours of basics,' Barrie reminded Edy, which did not cheer up his irritated pal.

*　　*　　*　　*　　*　　*

Just when Edy thought there was plenty of time to plan a different operation, disaster struck Music Club—well, not exactly a disaster if you weren't a part of the Violin

Club. It was more of a disaster to the six girls under the supervision of the violinist, now ex-violinist.

The awful news came just weeks after Mr Michael Raphael was recruited to the Music Club. It was coincidentally a gloomy morning when Mr Joseph Matthew, the stern character, announced the resignation of Mr Pale-Faced Violinist. And everyone knew precisely what explanation Mr Joseph would give to explain the untimely resignation of the violin teacher—the most vague explanation. 'Because of certain unforeseen reasons, Mr Coogy Cal, the violin teacher, has resigned from his post. We wish him all the very best for his future endeavours.'

At this point, every curious student knew who they would go to, to find out the actual reason of Mr Coogy Cal's resignation—the most authenticated source that they could rely on was Miss Ashria Kaum. She was well aware that revealing the true reason would not possibly cause any sort of trouble to the management or to the Chambers of Principal Authority, given the fact that nobody appreciated Mr Cal to such an extent that his resignation would spark mayhem within the school premises.

The only ones who were concerned about resignation were the six violin learners that included Troniya and

Mable. The management was all the more happy that they could cut down on his salary, and the other members of the Music Club were relieved that they had finally got rid of the face that that suppressed their enthusiasm.

After the management learnt that there were only a merry six violin learners, they no longer searched for another music teacher. Mr Joseph too agreed with the management's decision, given the fact that it was rather impractical to find a violin-only expert.

After three days, the students, mostly the senior ones, got their curiosity quenched when Miss Ashria, after much research and eavesdropping on the members of CPA, revealed the actual reason for Mr Cal's resignation. The pathetic reason was as pathetic as those explanations given by Allen to the annoying questions of the newcomers.

Ghosts! Apparently, Mr Pale-Faced Violinist had chanced upon two ghosts when he was taking his usual walk late after dinner. His late-night walks resembled that of the watch guards of the school, who would stroll across the vast grounds of the premises at unusual timings.

'See, I wasn't lying about seeing ghosts,' Allen confidentially said to Jade as Miss Ashria Kaum revealed the reason. 'There's the proof.'

Jade, who had shifted his bed to a more populated corner of the dormitory got goosebumps all over on hearing the reason for the resignation.

'That's absurd. He must have strolled across the deserted ends of the premises,' Edy said, as he heard Allen, 'and it appears he imagined those two ghostlike things, out of trepidation.'

'I wonder if those two ghosts are still in service.' Barrie mockingly said, 'I would love to personally thank them for showing up that night.'

'Do you think they saw Mr Cal? What if they had seen Mr Cal?' Jade asked, feeling awful for the violinist.

'If they happened to have seen his pale face, I'm pretty sure they would have submitted their resignation as well,' Barrie said, after which bursts of laughing erupted from those who heard his joke.

Clusters of possible explanations erupted among the puzzled students.

'He must have seen those church owls and mistaken them for ghosts,' Rodney put forward his view.

'Or maybe it's the ignis fatuus effect,' Jeoff fearfully said.

'You mean will-o'-the-wisp?' Daffney, after overhearing Jeoff's possible explanation, asked.

'Yup,' Jeoff confirmed, 'also called the jack-o'-lantern.'

'Can't be,' Celia resisted, 'probably one of those ball lightning.'

'I strongly feel it's got something to do with foxfire.' Reny added her views.

'I agree,' Barrie supported her, 'given that there is plenty of decaying wood and a dozen varieties of fungi species in the corners of the premises.'

'Or probably the fireflies effect,' Edy added to the group chat; only Barrie and Celia agreed.

On the following Saturday afternoon, the six violin learners were called to the Chambers of Principal Authority. After a brief explanation of the management's decision, Mr Joseph admitted that there would be no violin teacher to assist the girls anymore. In return, Mr Joseph offered the tiny group two choices, one fairly obvious and the other bizarre:

a. To shift to another instrument that Mr Raphael could assist with

b. To aid the academic staff with the academic stuff that included a lot of paperwork and assisting the Portions Planning Committee as well as the Examination Conducting Committee.

The second choice was named Academic Club, as called by Mr Joseph. The newly created so-called Academic Club came into effect when several indolent teachers had earlier insisted on creating an academic club, which was deliberately denied by Mr Joseph Matthew. Now that the lazy teachers had another opportunity, they swiftly put the request back on the principal's desk, for the second time. Even though Mr Joseph was against it, he chose to give the violin learners the option of joining the Academic Club.

Finally, through Mable, Edy learnt that both Troniya and Mable had chosen the Academic Club over the first option. Edy didn't dare to question further as to why they had chosen the Academic Club. For the next three days, Edy was angry at the lazy group of teachers, which included Mr Samuel, Mr Paul, Mr Jerald, and Miss Belinda—the creators of the Academic Club. Had they not been so lazy and had they not requested for the Academic Club, Troniya would have still been a part of the Music Club— more fortunately, not learning violin anymore.

Edy grudgingly tore the list of opening statements that he had prepared. He realized that without having a common bridge between the two of them, he could not possibly approach Troniya without arousing suspicion in her as well as the curious onlookers. The only chance of a potential situation to make a casual encounter that he had, had been lost.

With life getting back to normality at MPS, Edy had nothing to cheer about, except his newfound interest—guitars.

'It's the easiest instrument of all,' Mr Raphael said to his eight-member team, 'You can get fluent with guitars in less than a year.'

Edy knew it was easier said than done. He had a hard time remembering the names of the numerous different chords; so did the others. Mr Raphael also made his pupils remember the names of the six strings, starting from the fattest one—E A D G B E, respectively.

The guitar learners were tediously trying to learn how different symbols that were used along with the basic notes were pronounced. Some of the fundamental symbols included (#) pronounced *sharp*, (m) pronounced *minor*, (b) pronounced *flat*, (#m) which was a combination of the two and pronounced *sharp minor*, (M) pronounced *major*, (sus) which was short for *sustained*, (bm) was again the combination of the two and pronounced *flat minor*. The more difficult ones to play were the simplest ones to remember, like 9–7–6–13, etc.

These symbols, as Mr Raphael precisely said, could not be used on their own, but to be combined with the basic seven notes—A B C D E F G.

So if (#) was combined with any of the basic notes, for example (G#), it was pronounced *G sharp*. Similarly, adding m with any basic note, like (Am), was pronounced *A minor*.

A few of the easy ones that the guitar learners could easily remember were:

A# (A sharp), Bb (B flat), Cm (C minor), D`sus (D sustained), E#m (E sharp minor), F (simply F or F Major), Gbm (G flat minor), B`9 (B nine), C`7 (C seven), Db (D flat), and Abm (A flat minor).

*   *   *   *   *   *

The First Realization

Tuesday, 10 October 2006

*T*wo weeks into October, the midterm exams did become a reality, against the wishes of four-hundred-odd students. It was the first paper, English, the one that was handled by Miss Andrella for the senior boys. There was hardly any trepidation seen among the exam writers in the exam hall. It wasn't English that was a real challenge for the major lot, but papers like mathematics, science, history, and computers. The more difficult part in history was to remember the historically significant dates along with the reason why the dates had become so noteworthy.

The top five reasons why the dates had become so significant, according to Allen, the self-proclaimed expert in the subject, were:

a. A famous personality had been born / had died / had been killed.

b. A major invention/discovery had been made, accidentally or otherwise.

c. A major treaty/pact had been signed between several countries, like peace treaties or setting up of global organizations such as peace organizations, health organizations, etc.

d. Some or the other country had been invaded and/or captured and/or liberated.

e. A major global revolution had taken place, like the Industrial Revolution, green revolution, or technological revolution.

The copyists' groups in different senior grades, including grade 10, had already gotten ready to put their new copying tricks into practice. The most recent trick of the copyists was the 'hole in the tie' trick. Someone in the group with a chunk of luck had noticed a tiny gap at the broader end of the tie, which was made bigger by loosening the stitches. The copying chits were then folded flat and carefully sneaked into the gap. Even though the poor quality of the stitching was to be blamed, the copyists never missed out on trying and finding new methods of sneaking the chits. This was probably the cleverest method that anyone had come across in the history of MPS. The major assurance for using this trick widely came from the fact that no inspecting teacher had ever suspected anyone to sneak in chits into the examination hall with the help of school ties. It was like smuggling gold bars concealed in silver bars. No inspecting officer would have ever said, 'Wait, I sense gold is being smuggled in these silver bars.'

Likewise, there was no single incident when an inspecting teacher had suddenly paused by a suspecting student, saying, 'Please untie your tie, I sense there are concealed chits inside.' That had never happened. All that the inspecting squad bothered to inspect were the trouser pockets (lame), shirt pockets (lame), underneath the shoes (clever), inside the socks (clever), beneath the collar (clever), and of course in the stationery boxes (again, lame).

The other most reliable method of sneaking in chits until the previous year was the 'pen with refill' trick. A clever kid in grade 7 had come up with the bright idea of rolling the copying chits onto the thin plastic refill and sliding it back into the pen body. This trick had spread like wildfire on a sunny afternoon.

Sadly, the 'pen with refill' method was busted by Mr Hal, when he was inspecting the students of grade 8. A careless and excited student had rolled the chit in a pen that had a transparent body. Apparently the copying chit was clearly visible to Mr Hal even though his eyesight was not as good as it used to be a decade ago. Generally the users of 'pen with refill' method had to make sure to use a covered pen. The more expensive pens were typically covered by a layer of non-transparent plastic with the name of the manufacturer and the model of the pen usually printed on it.

'The unlucky grade 8 kid must have used a cheaper version,' many students thought when they heard about the dire news, 'which is why it didn't have the protective transparent layer to conceal the hidden chits.' That was how the 'pen with refill' method had been put to rest by the copyists' groups in all grades, mostly grades 6 to 12.

The pre-midterm examination ended after a straining two weeks and packing began for the four-week-long holidays. In about three hours, the grounds of MPS would be deserted, with no one loitering around for the next month.

The parking grounds of MPS quickly filled up as cars and minivans zoomed in through the huge red-painted metal gates.

As Edy and Barrie waited back at the entrance of the parking bay, the sight of a man approaching the dormitories caught the bursting attention of the onlookers.

He was in his forties and had a well-built physique that brought out an elegant manly look. He was clean-shaven and looked perfectly organized. His hair was well groomed like that of a perfect gentleman; his clothes were a carefully ironed, tucked-in white shirt with matching black trousers. The black leather shoes he wore were shinier than those of Mr Joseph. His steadfast conduct indicated he was in some serious post.

'I wonder who that man is,' Edy said as both continuously gazed at him with utmost attention to his mannish demeanour and spruce outfit. The stern expression on him was more conspicuous than all the other out-of-the-ordinary traits that he had put up.

'Who could he possibly be?' Edy asked again before a loud horn at the school gates grabbed his attention. A second after Edy turned back to the gates, Barrie nudged his pal.

'Edy, look,' Barrie said as the man stopped right outside the doors of the senior girls' dormitory.

'Troniya's dad?' Edy asked, astounded at seeing Troniya fondly hugging and talking to him.

'Probably,' Barrie said, 'I wonder what profession he's into.'

No spoken reply came from Edy. They both stood and gazed from across the slowly filling up parking bay.

'He must certainly be a police officer,' Barrie said after a deeper analysis of the man whom they now knew was Troniya's dad, 'or a prominent lawyer or probably a major adjudicator in the court of law.'

Barrie paused to think of more professions that suited his appearance, and a moment later, another girl from a junior grade joined the two.

'Now who could that be?' Edy asked his thinking pal.

'Troniya's sister.' Barrie revealed, 'That's the only possible explanation for the hugging from the young girl.'

'Are you sure?' Edy asked.

'There's an uncanny resemblance between the two,' Barrie started to point out, 'fair complexion, similar noses, straight hair, body weight, dressing style.'

'I agree,' Edy interrupted, 'but a police officer?'

'More likely a senior police officer' Barrie corrected.

'That does scare me,' Edy confessed with a terrified tone.

'Are you sure you want to continue with whatever you planned to continue with?' Barrie asked, knowing all that Edy had been doing to get in touch with Troniya.

After a momentary silence, Edy dimly whispered, 'Only time will tell.'

A week into the one-month-long break, Edy realized he was not feeling quite normal. After explaining it to Barrie over a one-hour phone conversation, the latter said that he was suffering from the 'missing someone' syndrome or MSS for short. Barrie also explained that it could not be countered until and unless Edy could see 'someone' again.

'That's three weeks to go' Edy cried to his analyzer friend.

'You have to live with it,' Barrie firmly said. 'There's no other way.'

As Edy aimlessly sat in his room that very evening, the sharp voice of the newsreader floated through the wooden door.

'The weather continued to race downstream and so did atmospheric humidity in several parts of the country. The current temperature in the city stands at 16 degrees Celsius. The bitterly cold weather has given rise to black ice in some of the neighbouring cities.

'The general public has been constantly warned to avoid long exposure to the breezy cold air.

Dr Moon, the weather forecast expert and the head of the National Weather Forecasting Department, has warned of a severe fall wind in the next three weeks. He, however, said that there may not be any snow shower.

'Several reports came in today that claimed to have witnessed multiple fogbows in and around the city limits. The formation of ground fog has given rise to speculations of a severe fog cover in the near future. The hygrometer has been indicating a declining humidity level and the same is to be expected to continue for the next two months.

'Most of the northern part of the country has remained mainly cloudy since last Monday, followed by dense fog that has reduced the visibility to a mere twenty meters.

'The meteorology department has linked these sudden changes in the atmospheric temperature to the increasing greenhouse gases and the ever-growing population.

The department has also come forward to do extensive research on the reports provided by the National Weather Forecasting Department.'

The news was strange, the kind that Edy had never heard before, while his dad stared at the newsreader, already feeling the tingly prick of the coming winter.

The next day, Edy decided to shake the MSS or 'missing someone' syndrome off his mind. He insisted to his mom that he would want to help her out with the household shopping and quickly grabbed the shopping list.

The train arrived at the eastern station and Edy sat at one corner. The unpleasantly cold wind had chilled the glass windows.

Soon he was on his way to Mr Samuel's supermarket. On the way, he came across many newly established outlets that didn't exist the last time he had been there. There was a new vacuum cleaner showroom, a tiny bookstore, a stationery shop at the corner end and a beauty salon above the grand old furniture store from which they had purchased their new furniture set last summer.

On reaching Mr Samuel's supermarket, Edy rolled down the list and took along with him a metal trolley from the trolley stand. After having strolled different aisles, he had finally gotten all that the list contained, including his dad's choice of spiced cream soy sauce and stuffed olives. The installation of anti-theft devices at the two exits, several rotating CCTVs fitted on the ceiling, and the newly laid wooden flooring did imply one thing for sure—Mr Samuel's business was at its peak.

On his way back, Edy came across Buguel's bookstore, a bookstore that was owned by his friend Keli Mike. He paused opposite to number 73, next to the personal security services and detective agency enterprise office. Buguel's bookstore was known for the variety of books that they had in store. It was the best bookstore ever since Matche's bookstore went out of business a decade ago.

On the display window was the latest collection that was in store. Just as Edy leapt in to get a closer look at the bright yellow book on theories of the universe, a familiar voice called out to him.

'Could that be you, Edy?' Keli Mike asked, popping his head out of his office window.

Edy smiled back. 'Could be me or a perfectly designed body double.' Both shared a hearty laugh before Mike invited Edy, 'Hop in, let me show you our latest collection.'

Why not? Edy thought, *I might as well buy a book to keep me busy.*

*   *   *   *   *   *

Back at Barrie's, his mom had his favourite dish prepared—salmon. The smell of the large, silvery fish that had been fried with butter tickled his heightened sense of smell.

The dining table was arranged and Barrie's parents had occupied a part of the table. The scent candles were lit and the melted wax rolled down, producing a fabulous aroma which made a perfect environment to gulp down the hot, juicy serving. Barrie made himself comfortable on the chair that he always argued was the perfect dining spot.

'Thanks for the salmon, Mom,' Barrie delightedly said as his mom served him fried salmon and a portion of steamed asparagus prepared with roasted pine nuts.

Soon after Barrie gulped down his first piece of the salmon, the phone rang. The hollandaise sauce was next to treat his craving taste buds. The ringing continued. 'I'll take it,' Barrie insisted and forcefully raced to the other end of the hall and picked up the receiver.

'Hello?'

'Barrie!' the voice on the other end called out.

'Edy?' Barrie asked, 'What's up?'

'Limerence.'

At once, Barrie understood what Edy was trying to put across. His rapid reply and a vexed tone did suggest he was willing to have a rather serious conversation of what to do next.

'Wow!' Barrie said rather excitedly. 'Wasn't expecting that, not this quickly.'

'I know, I shouldn't have read that book from Mike's earlier today,' Edy dejectedly admitted.

'You read a book from Mike's?' Barrie asked, 'What kind of a book?'

'Romantic fiction.'

*   *   *   *   *   *

The Prick of Winter

*I*t was in the month of December that the schoolgoing boys tiptoed stealthily and sneaked towards the door on which one would find a signboard with a scary-looking human skull and crossbones and the words THE WARD OF MISCHIEVOUS ELEMENTS carved on it. They would desperately knock on the door to find out the mischievous elements that were kept in reserve for them to experiment on. On the other side of the door was the wicked Lady Winter, waiting for disobedient students to enter the room filled with abundant recipes of mischief.

The prick of winter is all that we are talking about. It's the immoral spell that Lady Winter ruthlessly casts on those who are on the brink of doing unusual things. The more vulnerable the student is, the more the effect of the merciless spell. Lady Winter's freezing winter spell would only boost up the natural ability of schoolgoing boys to get into troubles, when they were already gifted with natural instincts of naughtiness.

Coincidentally, the winter of the year 2006 was particularly out of the ordinary when compared to the statistics of the previous years. There was a drastic change in the temperature levels right at the beginning of December. The extremely chill weather not only indicated that Lady Winter and the prick of her spell were more powerful than ever, but also that the intensity of the unusual activity that the spellbound students performed would be dangerously bizarre. The intransigent spell, once cast upon the vulnerable student, tended to have long-term effects or until their illegal activities were busted by the authorities.

Two such students who were highly pricked by Lady Winter's cold spell were Eric Reez and Ray Anderson, both of whom already belonged to the 'Up to No Good' group of grade 10.

Eric Reez and Ray Anderson, the two occupants of row 4, desk 4, for a while now had been observing an odd activity at row 4, desk 3. A thick, black-leather-finished book in Troniya's desk was what had caused the curiosity in their nerves to quiver. The secretive way in which the owner wrote in that book every alternate day or so was what triggered them to spy on it all the more. Adding fuel to the reason for their ill prying was the fact that nobody had ever laid their hands on that book except Troniya.

What could it possibly contain? Eric and Ray thought about it rather seriously.

'Maybe it's a magic book,' Ray Anderson suggested after they had an argument about the possible contents of the eye-catching book. 'It might contain secrets and magic spells to score high points.'

'Don't be ridiculous.' Eric Reez snorted.

'How else does she do it?' cried Ray.

'I don't know,' Eric admitted his ignorance.

'I'm sure she uses some kind of sorcery related to academics,' Ray stupidly said.

'Are you sure?' Eric asked doubtfully.

'More than just sure,' Ray assured him. 'After we have learnt those magic tricks, we will take everyone by surprise by scoring the highest in the midterm exams.'

'Wow, that's intriguing,' Eric said.

'Eric Reez – rank 1, Ray Anderson – rank 2,' Ray muttered cheerfully.

'Woooo . . . I like the sound of that,' Eric said, rubbing his warm hands.

'Then let's do it,' Ray suggested.

'Or maybe it's just the important lecture points that she notes down at the end of each day,' Eric dully guessed.

'Why would she write it in such a secretive manner if it was merry lecture points?' Ray asked.

Eric gave it deep thought without reaching an explanatory conclusion.

'Also why would she not let anyone read it, not even Irennica, her bench mate?' Ray put forward his doubts.

'And she writes only during the last five minutes of the evening prep.' Eric joined Ray in questioning.

'Exactly!' Ray jumped in excitement. 'That book contains something that she doesn't want any of us to know.'

'You're right!' Eric ultimately agreed, and they both made their immoral move as they approached row 4, desk 3.

Troniya's desk was painstakingly arranged in the perfect order, like any other girl's in the class. At the bottom of the arranged pile of books was the large, thick, black-leather-finished book that the intruders were looking for.

Ray made himself comfortable on the bench, while Eric stood by him. After they had sighted the helpless book, Ray gently lifted the grade 10 subject-related books and carefully withdrew the leather-finished book underneath and placed it on his lap.

'What?' both the intruders exclaimed spontaneously, surprised on seeing the title of the book.

The words 'PERSONAL DIARY – 2006' were imprinted on the smooth leather surface. They briefly exchanged knowing looks and Ray held it more fondly like a stolen diamond.

If someone happened to see the diary, they would feel that the diary was boasting of itself, boasting of being someone's personal diary. It looked like the book showed off pride and self-dignity for being used by none but Troniya. And the two combined words 'personal diary' were more intriguing than any other words put together, for they caused a desperate, imperishable zeal in others to trespass on the diary's contents.

'It's a personal diary,' Ray said gently, feeling the golden carvings with his fingers, still not sure if he should go ahead and open it.

'Open it!' Eric insisted, his widened eyes locked on the book.

'No, this isn't right,' Ray whispered guiltily. 'We shouldn't be doing this.'

'Why not?' Eric restlessly questioned his guilt-filled companion.

'I don't know. I don't feel good about opening it,' Ray admitted politely.

'You are as pathetic as you can get,' Eric spat and threw his hands on the book, which accidentally opened it and the first page revealed contents that caught their utmost attention.

WARNING! THIS DIARY SOLELY BELONGS TO ME—TRONIYA. NO ONE WILL, WITHOUT MY PRIOR PERMISSION, READ IT OR EVEN MISPLACE IT. IF ANYONE DISOBEYS AND DARES TO MOVE FURTHER, BEWARE! FOR THEY WILL INDEFINITELY SUFFER MY CURSE

OF POVERTY AND SICKNESS AS IT WILL BEFALL ON THEM, AFTER WHICH THEY WILL BEG ME FOR MERCY, WHICH I MAY DENY. SO THE BEST OPTION YOU HAVE RIGHT NOW IS TO CLOSE THIS DIARY AND PUT IT BACK WHERE YOU KNOWINGLY OR UNKNOWINGLY FOUND IT.

Eric's eyes widened further in excitement while Ray swallowed hard, feeling his guilt run down his spine.

'I told you I had a bad feeling about this,' Ray pointed out.

'Shut up, Ray,' Eric said with an evil grin. 'We have found a personal diary—we should read it.'

'I don't feel very moral about your plan.' Ray shook his head. 'It's wrong to read others' personal matters.'

'Okay, you be off while I read,' Eric said and snatched the book from Ray's hands.

'Okay, wait!' Ray hesitated for a brief moment and swallowed again. 'This will stay only between us, right?'

'Of course,' Eric mischievously nodded and carefully put back the diary on the desktop, 'unless you intend on revealing it to the others.'

On the page that Ray turned, it was written:

Date: 8 January, 2006

Dad was dreadfully upset the whole week. His sincerity and hard work at work has not been acknowledged by his managers. He isn't very happy with the company's appraisal methods as well. The incentives are barely noticeable in his pay account. The worst part is the health toll that his job is talking on him. Mom is worried, so are sis and I.

'She has a sister?' Eric interrupted.

Ray nodded swiftly. 'I heard her talking to Irennica the other day. She's in grade 5.' They both nodded and continued.

Mom suggested to cancel the dinner that Dad had planned for their wedding anniversary. I and sis agreed, given that it wasn't the perfect time to celebrate. But dad was too loving and caring. He took us out for dinner and we all spent a lovely evening that evening. It was a memorable family outing.

'Turn,' Eric interrupted again. 'Nothing interesting here.'
Ray agreed and acted accordingly.

A few pages further, Ray stopped.

Date: 16 March 2006

This was the day when dad learnt about the
unethical practices that his company had been
secretively carrying out. It shook his moral values.
The one word that he cannot bear to withstand—
unlawful. Being an ex-serviceman, that did
make a great impact on his future decisions. His
willingness to quit the job was next to nothing. It's
only a matter of days until he finds a new job in
a new company that does business abiding to the
laws of the country. I still wonder if quitting the
navy was a good idea.

'Her dad had been with the navy?' Eric asked, his voice
suddenly less excited than before.

'That's what this diary says,' Ray pointed out.

'No wonder she gets top scores in all the subjects,'
Eric reminded.

'One of the many effects of having a navy dad,' Ray replied musingly and turned a few more pages.

> Date: 24 April 2006
>
> Why are Mom's relatives so annoying? Not that Dad's relatives are any better! For once they won't stop enquiring about me. I say, 'Yes, I was the topper in grade 6, 7, 8, and 9,' and they ask me, '*How?*' How lame? Argh! What were they expecting me to say anyway?

'See?' Ray interrupted. 'How the profession of a dad can have a direct proportional positive impact on the child's academic performance.'

Without giving a reply, Eric moved further. He wasn't very excited to know what he already knew or what he could fairly expect.

As Eric feebly turned the pages, something familiar seemed to have caught Ray's attention, as he held on to a particular page, abruptly bringing Eric's action to a halt.

'What's the matter?' Eric asked impatiently.

'Look,' Ray pointed out the word that had caught his attention. 'There's something written about Miss Andrella.'

On the page that Ray held, it was written:

Miss Andrella, along with the other staff members and members of the Portions Planning Committee and Examination Conducting Committee were very pleased to have me and Mable in the newly created Academic Club!

I so wanted to learn violin, but destiny had created a different path for me to continue my journey. And what a nonsensical reason Mr Coogy Cal had given to reason his resignation. Ghosts! Couldn't he have come up with a more realistic reason? Or was it true that he really happened to have experienced some sort of paranormal activity?

'Now this is where it gets interesting,' Eric muttered with a mischievous smile.

'Let's read from the start of where matters relating to MPS begin,' Ray suggested.

A few pages backwards and they both knew where the part relating to the school began.

Date: 10 June 2006

A new school, a new twist in life, a new town, new friends, teachers, surroundings: doesn't feel exactly the way I had imagined it to be. Maybe I should give it some more time. It's just been a week. Dad, why did you have to join a company that keeps imposing work transfers every year or so? Had it not been for the new job at Centronites, we all could have still been together, in our own hometown. I'm not complaining. I would sacrifice anything for you, like you have always done for us.

'How sweet!' Ray said as he felt the strong dad–daughter relations and the everlasting unbreakable bond between the family members.

Things have taken an unexpected turn in our lives. I and sis in MPS, you in Centronites, and Mom back in hometown. But that won't change us from who we are. We always love each other and distance doesn't make an impact on the might of our family bond. Until the reunion of our family, I shall wait, wait for us to be together again like the good old times.

*   *   *   *   *   *

The wicked Lady Winter was back on her frozen feet, loitering around to find any potential victims who were on the verge of falling into traps and doing mischievous acts like Ray and Eric were.

She did come across Edy and his vulnerable state, which was very conspicuous to her. She pointed her wand and tried to cast the wicked pricking spell, which did not happen. She realized her powers were not fully functional as they were not as strong as she wanted them to be in order to be able to cast her spell on strong-minded people. It was only the dawn of December.

As decided earlier, Edy and Barrie revealed the former's big secret to the members of their group—Mable, Celia, Jade, and Allen. Though Edy was very reluctant to reveal it to Allen, he finally did when the forcefulness of Barrie turned unbearable. Edy only hoped Allen would not make the former his victim of humour over and over again.

Throughout the revelation, Allen thought he was being tricked into some kind of practical joke. What was harder was giving him solid proof that Edy was planning on proposing to Troniya, the proof which Allen had been demanding from the beginning of the big revelation.

'There is no solid proof, Allen,' Barrie whined when Allen, for the fifth time, asked for it. 'It's not a business deal.'

At the end, Allen had one word to say to the revealers: 'Liars.' He repeated the word thrice before he said, 'I don't believe a word you say.'

It wasn't very easy to convince Celia and Mable as well. But with Barrie's intervention, Celia believed, and with Celia's intervention, Mable did too. Of course that was after a lot of frowning and nail biting and several high-pitched *What*s.

After an intense discussion, Edy and Barrie isolated the idea of creating another common bridge. They both agreed that time was running out and that the options they had to create a common bridge were almost nil.

The concluding decision involved intervention by Mable, Troniya's only partner in the Academic Club.

The midterm exam was fast approaching; so was the harshness of the winter. Temperature at MPS drastically dropped overnight on 2 December 2006. The weather had turned harsh, wicked, and ruthless.

As Edy read the newspaper the following Sunday afternoon, he felt a sharp freezing sensation run through his veins instantly. The oddity of the news article in the weather column caught everyone's attention as they gathered around him to have quick statistical information on the current temperature levels as well as the forecasted ones. The weather report on 3 December 2006 read:

There has been a sudden fall in the temperature levels throughout the country as well as in the neighbouring countries. The thermometer indicated a sharp 14 degrees Celsius fall in the last twenty-four hours. The National Weather Forecasting Department head and weather researcher Dr Moon has warned of harsher weather in the near future. The common public is not expected to stray outdoors from 9 p.m. to 9 a.m. until further notice is issued by the Weather Forecasting Department. Dr Moon has said that the temperature during the nights could fall anywhere between 2 degrees Celsius to 4 degree Celsius, which he admits is sufficient to cause hypothermia if exposed for a long duration.

Dr Moon also suggested that the common public keep their room heaters switched on throughout the night to prevent extreme chillness that could again cause rashes from exposure to severe cold. The humidity level has plunged to 22 per cent, which indicates that the atmospheric air is exceedingly dry. Together with the freezing cold weather, this could easily cause cold, flu, skin rashes, hypothermia, etc.

'The humidity levels are further expected to drop to about 10 per cent to 12 per cent,' Dr Moon said at the National Weather Forecasting Department headquarters.

The public is expected to be outdoors only if dressed in multilayer woollen clothes and heat-insulated jackets and generous use of cold creams or anti-dryness creams.

'I have never come across a weather statistic like this one in my entire forty years of service at the National Weather Forecasting Department,' Dr Moon had posted on the department's website.

The weather did get cruel as predicted by Dr Moon. The dry, harsh, brutal wind knifed through the buildings and trees at MPS. No amount of cold creams, skin moisturizers, or winter creams was of any use. The only warmth that they got was from the newly installed low-cost room heaters and from the smoky, bubbling hot water during morning and evening baths. The woollen clothes were now out of the cupboards, covering every inch of skin that kept the students warm.

The junior-grade students were so heavily clothed that they were hardly recognizable. The only part that was spared was their eyes, covering which would make them artificially blind and many would end up crashing into the electric poles or the huge rain trees that are scattered all over the place.

The wicked Lady Winter was back; she was more powerful than ever as the winter grew to its harshest point. Her next target was a vulnerable Edy, who was already at her doorstep that had the skull and crossbones sign and the words THE WARD OF MISCHIEVOUS ELEMENTS carved on it, the same door which Eric Reez and Ray Anderson had knocked on earlier that winter.

The unforgiving Lady Winter was more than happy to receive Edy as she peeped through the spying hole on her door. No sooner had he stepped in, than an unbreakable spell of the prick of the winter was cast upon him. The frozen, pointy, magical wand penetrated deep into his skin, releasing the cold prick into his bloodstream. Like a grimy virus at work, the prick spread to each of his billion cells.

The more the prick spread, the more eager he was to make his first move to approach Troniya. The force that he had lacked when he made his first try back at the Music Club now came flooding towards him, like an unsuspected tsunami. Even though he could feel every bit of the prick of the spell that was cast upon him, he was oblivious of it, for it had come in the natural form, the form of weather—the winter.

Springing one last evil laugh on her new victim, the evil Lady Winter disappeared into thin air to find more vulnerable victims.

Backed by the prick of Lady Winter's spell, Edy finally approached Mable, who in turn was to convince Troniya to meet him personally. Mable swiftly denied his perilous request, for she feared the dire consequences that she might have to face, should the plan go wrong. She admitted she would have done it, had it been any other girl in the class. Troniya was way too serious a student, way too sturdy, studious to accept such a request.

'What if she escalates this matter to Miss Andrella?' Mable courteously asked. 'Or even worse, to Mr Joseph?'

At first Edy denied that Troniya would take the matter so seriously. But after Mable revealed the prior profession of her dad, he sat dumbfounded.

Ex-serviceman? He's been with the navy? Edy thought, biting his thumbnail and panicking, *Would she have gotten the strict, lawful, law-filled, anti-illegal genes from her dad?*

He certainly knew that 'talking personally' was not considered as a very legal/moral/ethical act at MPS; so did every other student. The relevant warning that Mr Joseph had given to the students on the first day came back to him instantaneously.

But wait, wasn't the wicked Lady Winter searching for a potential victim? One whip from the icy wand and

Mable was bestowed with the winter spell. At once Mable agreed to deliver his message to Troniya. She too, like Edy, was oblivious of the effects of the wintry spell. The invisible Lady Winter did keep an eye on Edy and his desperate actions that would ultimately lead him to the pit of plight.

The very next day, Mable had planned on conveying the message to Troniya. She waited for the perfect time to make her move. It was undoubtedly the ten-minute coffee break. As the coffee break bells went off, all the students of grade 10 dispersed while Mable quickly held back Lady Winter's subsequent victim.

'Mable! What's the matter?' Troniya asked with a befuddled smile.

'Um . . . er . . . Troniya, er . . . I . . .' Mable mumbled rapidly, 'I don't how to put this . . . er . . .'

'It's okay, tell me, what's up?' Troniya asked with a slight suspicion added to her confused smile.

'Um . . . It's a request . . . er . . . from someone . . .' Mable hesitated to add a name. 'Someone who wishes to meet you personally.'

'Meet me?' Troniya inquired perplexedly, 'Personally?'

'Umm . . . Yes . . . Yes . . . meet you . . . per- . . . personally.' Mable hesitantly ended the sentence.

Troniya frowned on hearing Mable's words for the second time.

'Who?' she asked curiously, though not excitedly.

'Um . . . Edy,' Mable apprehensively admitted with a sinking voice, which brought a spontaneous reply from the curious listener.

'What? Edy?' she asked with a more intense frown.

'Er . . . yes,' Mable said and waited for a reply. She was 99 per cent expecting Troniya to escalate this matter to Mr Joseph right away. If that happened, Mable knew exactly what she and Edy would have to face—indefinite suspension.

'Why does *he* want to speak to *me*?' Troniya asked impertinently, laying a lot of emphasis on the words *he* and *me*.

'I don't exactly know,' Mable admitted with lot of reluctance as she became nervous about her goading companions' subsequent actions. 'I was only requested to convey this message to you.'

Troniya was in bottomless thoughts while Mable desperately waited for a positive reply as she held on to her slipping hopes.

Standing invisibly next to the two concerned girls was the malevolent Lady Winter, who had been following Mable, who eventually led her to her next victim. With the glassy wand in her hand and a dreadful spell up her sleeve, the wicked Lady Winter unleashed her winter curse.

A second after the dire spell had been bestowed upon Troniya, she expressed her decision to agree to Mable's request.

'Okay, I will,' Troniya said, not knowing what had pushed her to agree to the risky request, 'but only after the midterm exams.'

The wicked Lady Winter strolled by, giving an evil laugh, for she was able to cast her cold prick spell on the girl who was nowhere near to the door of the Ward of Mischievous Elements.

Mable showed a sign of deep relief on hearing Troniya's acceptance.

Never mind, Mable thought as she went on to reveal the big surprise to Edy.

On hearing from Mable, Edy felt his heart bloom like a spring flower within. A profound sign of triumph fell upon his contented face.

Only three more weeks and the midterm exams will be over, he thought as Mable told him about the condition that Troniya had put forward. *And even better, I have got three weeks to plan.*

He wholeheartedly thanked Mable for the fruitful help that she had given by taking a huge risk.

Now that Troniya had agreed to meet Edy personally, he was not even concerned about the upcoming midterm exams that were due in a week's time. Meeting Troniya topped his list of Most Important Things to Be Presently Concerned About. Exams were almost at the bottom of the list, followed by the promise that was made to Mr Joseph a few months ago, when he was appointed the primary class representative of grade 10.

The five victims of Lady Winter's spell, Eric, Ray, Edy, Mable, and Troniya, were all in seventh heaven. *For now.*

The copyists group in the senior grades was back in form as the midterm exams commenced. This time there had been a more ingenious method of sneaking in the chits. It was known as the 'loose calculator' method. It was as simple as it sounded. Loosen all the screws of the calculator, carefully place the folded copying chits, and loosely tighten the gaps between the two plastic boards. This way the chits were hidden in the belly of the calculator.

No one was sure who had invented it, though there were several claims to the invention, probably to take credit. But whoever had done it, it was very obvious that the inventor of the calculator trick had spent a great deal of time fiddling with all the stationery products before having decided on the calculator.

To add to the misfortunes of the copyists' group, this method too was busted right on the third exam of the midterm, more intriguingly by the same person who had busted the 'pen with refill' trick—Mr Hal; that gave another reason for the copyists to hate him even more. The irony was that the teacher who could not tell a crow from a pigeon had busted almost half the tricks of the copyists' group.

It was Ray Anderson's foolishness that had led to the revelation of the 'loose calculator' method. The 'loose calculator' method had a rule of thumb as the 'pen with refill' trick had. The 'pen with refill' trick was not to be used with a pen that had a transparent cover. Likewise, the 'loose calculator' method was supposed to be used during papers that involved calculations, like mathematics, statistics, accountancy, etc. By this, the inspecting squad would not get suspicious on seeing a calculator. Ray had probably forgotten the rule of thumb as he had desperately sneaked in the chit-filled calculator to all the exams, even to those subjects that had nothing remotely to do with a calculator, like biology, English, and history.

A puzzled Mr Hal finally inspected Ray's calculator, when, for the third day in a row, he had brought in the not-required stationery. It was the history paper. Not that Mr Hal was dumb, but it didn't demand the inspecting squad to have a 100+ IQ to sense the oddness on Ray's desk. Busted. There were three chits folded in different shapes. It was most likely to identify which one contained what information. The wording was so tiny and painstakingly written that Mr Hal had to read the contents with the help of a giant magnifier.

*   *   *   *   *   *

It was the last paper of midterm and all that Edy could think of in the exam hall was the fact that it was his big day—meeting Troniya for the first time. A little less than a thousand questions kept luring him into daydreaming during the final exam. *What do I tell her? Should I reveal the true reason for requesting her to meet me personally? Will I be able to do it? Even if I do, what would be her reaction? Will she be maddened? What if it's a big no-no? What do I do then? Should I keep pestering her against her wishes? Or should I just forget everything and move on? Will I be able to do that?* Ever?

Panic rapidly started to reside in him as he waited back in the empty class as planned earlier. It was his first actual meeting with Troniya and not like any of those hundreds of imaginary meetings that he had had during his daydreams. Butterflies hipped and hopped and mopped in his tummy as he hurriedly walked from one end to the other. Nerves electrified, ears turned hot, feet became cold, heart thumped loud, and palms turned sweaty.

Wait! Sweaty palms! Edy thought bringing his galloping walk to an abrupt halt. *What if I were to shake hands with her?* he thought, and an expression of disgust took over the anxiety-filled face. He quickly washed his hands with the freezing-cold water and rushed back to the deserted class, wiping off the wetness on his trousers and school tie.

Not moments later, he heard footsteps erupting from the empty, noiseless corridor. *Is it her? Or someone else?* Edy thought as he kept fumbling with his tie. The noise of the soft footsteps grew louder as they got nearer.

I'm so dead were the last words he could think of before the B-door cracked open on the other side.

Troniya! he thought as though he was being surprised.

As Troniya entered the hall, Edy promptly stopped fumbling with his tie. The sweat on his palms magically reappeared.

'Um . . . hi!' he hesitantly greeted her. His heart pounded at a hundred and twenty.

Damn it! Edy thought restlessly as he felt his bodily functions were nearly double of what he had experienced back at the Music Club.

'Hi . . .' Troniya replied as she stood at row 4, desk 1.

Edy's detective eyes took a cursory glance at his companion. She stood still, looking at the scribbled blackboard.

She's so pretty, he thought and took another sneaky peek at her before he noticed something very evident.

Something isn't right! Edy at once grasped the dull look on Troniya's face.

She had not shown any of the following signs: eagerness, excitement, happiness. Not even an artificial smile. All that was seen was a dull, gloomy, lifeless, murky, uninterested look.

'Um . . . what's . . . what's wrong with your eyes?' Edy asked, not able to suppress his curiosity.

Dimly shaking her head, she replied, still looking ahead, 'Nothing.'

'Are you sure?' Edy asked again, his eyes fixed on hers.

'I'm fine,' Troniya said quickly, taking the first glance at him before going back to reading the scribbled contents on the board. Her voice had evidently matched her gloomy appearance.

Something's certainly not right, he instantly thought as he heard her glum tone. *Has it got something to do with today's paper?*

Like always, his quick-witted brain worked out the math and gave him a speedy conclusive explanation.

No, that can't be true! he told his calculative brain. *It was English, the easiest of all. Why would she not do well in English?*

'Is it because you screwed up today's paper?' Edy hesitantly asked, which made him feel like an idiot.

I happened to have a friend of mine who, on a particular day, called me on my landline. Guess what his first question was '*Where are you?*' I was so tempted to give this answer: 'I'm out of country, on a vacation, *with my landline.*' Instead I gave him this: 'Where else do you think I am, you moron?'

Don't you feel like an idiot when you have tried asking a question for which the answer would have been so very obvious, like if you asked a priest if he was the one who performed the rituals/ceremonies at the church and the priest looks at you with a 'What do you think I do here?' expression, or if you could ever ask Albert Einstein if he could teach physics to grade 8 students. If Einstein would have been in a mood for fun, maybe his reply could have been 'Oh, I'm so sorry, but I teach only till grade 6. I haven't really touched upon the complex theories of the subject.'

But the next move that Troniya made took away Edy's 'I am such an idiot to have asked that question' feeling. She dimly nodded in agreement and turned towards the half shut B-door, looking at half the length of the B-corridor that was visible from her point of view. There was not a single soul moving about in the entire corridor. Deep silence fell.

I was right, Edy thought.

'How was it?' He shyly asked, 'I mean the paper, how bad was it?'

Troniya shook her head again without giving a spoken reply, still looking out of the half-opened door. Another minute of bottomless silence fell. Edy's addiction forced him to take several more sneaky peeks at her. Thankfully it was the side view, which made it all the more comfortable for him to look at her.

'Why did you want to meet me?' Troniya broke the utter silence and looked at Edy as she questioned him. Her voice was fairly brusque and husky.

Edy clearly knew she wasn't in a position to listen to anything let alone an abrupt proposal from a known stranger. The situation had turned against his expectations—cheerless, gloomy, and rough and a partner who was not exactly approachable at the moment.

'Um . . . no . . . nothing,' he stammered bit by bit as he struggled to come up with a cover story, which his quick-witted brain usually did in unforeseen situations like these. 'Nothing in particular . . . just . . . just casually . . . you see . . . like . . . like . . .'

Not a single cover story his now-slow and panicking brain could come up with as he stammered away.

'Is that all?' Troniya interrupted her confoundedly blabbering companion. She was glaring at him for a clear answer, which made Edy all the more perturbed to talk.

'Um . . . yes . . . er . . . that . . . er . . . that would be all.' He was baffled and took another cursory look at his pretty classmate.

'Can I leave now?' Troniya asked in a way that sounded more like a dour statement than a question.

'Um . . . yeah, sure . . . why not?' Edy unwillingly replied, not wanting to look at her anymore.

'Okay.' Troniya hastily said bye and looked at him for one last time before exiting through the B-door.

'Bye,' Edy whispered to himself, droopily staring at the cemented floor as the noise of her footsteps faded away into the emptiness of the corridor.

Once, one of my cousins, named Shilpa, in her twenties, was on her way to becoming a cooking expert. She prepared numerous types of dishes day in and day out. Not many days had passed when she first laid her hands on cooking a chicken dish. It was suppose to be a delicious, juicy, spiced chicken roast. I and my four other cousins were eagerly waiting with watering mouths, to quickly grab the scrumptious roast and gulp it down into our tummies. Several impatient minutes passed by as we sat next to the oven. The aroma of the half-cooked chicken intensified in the kitchen and tickled our noses endlessly. Our hunger drove us to make secretive attack plans to grab the dish once it was out or counter-attack plans if someone else laid their hands on the dish first.

Sadly when the oven was opened, we all ended up sitting in front of a burnt piece of meat. Bursts of laughter dominated the kitchen along with the pungent fumes that had gushed out of the oven.

Further investigation revealed that the oven was preset to a much higher degree of heat than required. What an embarrassing moment it was! For the next week, we made all possible sorts of cookery jokes on my 'chicken-roast expert' cousin. That was when she pledged never to try and prepare the flopped dish.

I'm pretty sure even you would have come across many such events, if not many, at least one. How bad would the situation get, when what you had expected turns out to be only something remotely unexpected. On top of that, there would be a participating audience to see your plight and mock you, just like we mocked my cousin.

Edy too was in this unexpected embarrassing situation, which was what drove him to take his next strong decision—to stop any and all possible plans to make any and all further moves to approach Troniya. That night as he lay on his bed, those scenes came back to him uncontrollably.

No! This is it, I'm not troubling her anymore, Edy thought and closed his eyes, which again took him back to the meeting scene.

*   *   *   *   *   *

The Unexpected Twist

'*I* am sorry, Edy,' Barrie said to his dismayed friend as they stayed back in the classroom, skipping the coffee break.

'It wasn't your fault,' Barrie assured his regretting bench mate over and over. 'Maybe what happened was destined to happen,'

'I guess that's what fate had planned for me, huh?' Edy said with a fake smile.

'I still don't understand the part where she gets moody,' Jade, who had occupied the empty row 1, desk 2 said, resting his thinking head on his palm as he rewound the scene narrated by Edy the previous evening.

'For God's sake, Jade,' Barrie whined, turning back to the new addition. 'She's a human too, and a girl at that, she would have feelings and emotions and girls get moody very quick,' Barrie continued, irritated, 'For the last time, please stop asking the same question over and over.'

'No, that's not what I meant,' Jade calmly defended himself and looked thoughtful as though he was trying to recollect his memory.

'What else could you possibly mean by that?' Barrie snorted as he stood up.

'You never listen to my full explanation, do you?' Jade snorted back.

'Explain!' Barrie demanded, folding his arms, which he did when he was either too interested or deeply challenged.

'It was the English paper, her best bet among many others,' Jade started to explain as he too stood up. 'She is undoubtedly the top scorer in English, literature in that is a cakewalk, why would she have not done well?' Jade paused as Barrie waited for the conclusion part while Edy sat still, uninterested in the conversation.

'There's only one plausible explanation to that,' Jade said.

'Explain,' Barrie demanded, his voice less haughty than earlier.

'She knew she had to meet Edy that evening,' Jade continued with a lot of keenness in his voice as he had finally gotten a chance to put forward his findings.

'She was obviously disturbed by the fact that a random classmate of hers had requested to meet her personally.

Jade briefly paused after he had made the last word sound quite fancy. 'That thought kept loitering in her mind during the exam, which had an impact, though not very strong, on her thinking capabilities and on completing the paper without any distractions.'

'It was a random request, from a random classmate,' Barrie whined with much concentration and his voice sounded like that of a child. 'Why would her thoughts get distracted in the first place even though she was well aware she had to meet him?'

'Two reasons: one, she was probably too scared to imagine the consequences that she might have to face, should anything go wrong,' Jade continued, revealing the final conclusion of his theory, 'and two, she probably likes Edy.'

Edy instantly turned back at Jade as the second probable conclusion had caught his attention or more precisely, the sentence felt good to listen to, like the soothing sound of the flute.

How I wish that were true, Edy thought while Barrie stood his ground, not accepting Jade's unofficial findings.

'But why would she get moody during the meet?' Barrie frowningly asked.

Edy sat like a child listening to a bedtime story, his ears craving to listen more of Jade's 'soothing to listen to, though they might not be true' findings.

'She probably prefers keeping her top rank to Edy,' Jade said, and Edy's widening eyes contracted. 'After all, she has a little seasoning of navy-ness in her family, what else do you expect?' Jade continued while Edy went back to staring the empty wall ahead, 'The flavour has to emit itself in the form of material evidence, in her case, the proficiency in academics.'

'I don't think what you have been saying all this while is true,' Barrie whined, unfolding his hands and going back to consoling his bench mate.

'Trust me, you guys,' Jade whiningly said. 'She definitely sees Edy as a compatible person, at least academically, but she is worried at the later consequences of facing the inevitable rage of her dad or the spitefulness of her mom, if her mom had been in the navy too.'

'Stop it,' Barrie said, which didn't have any effect on the self-taught detective.

'Her thoughts were distracted in the exam hall, because she was hesitant to meet him, just like Edy, and the fact that he had made an impact on her, irritated her to no end, which is why she was moody and all angry at him.'

'Stop it, will you?' Barrie said, keeping his calm. Jade continued as though Barrie was asking for more.

'She likes him, she just doesn't know it yet.' Edy looked at Jade again with an unsurpassable ray of hope passing across his lately pessimistic face.

'Enough, Jade,' Barrie finally broke out from the ball of rage that had been wobbling. 'Stop giving him false hopes—that's that least you could do.'

'No, I'm not,' Jade shot back. 'Do you have any idea how much I had to think it over to get it through?'

'If what you said were true, then why hasn't she apologized to him yet?' Barrie asked fumingly. 'Why hasn't she made the sorry move yet? Why would she be so stubborn if at all she had that spark in her, just like you said?'

Jade sat numb, not giving his enraged partner a suitable reply while Edy sighed and went back to keeping an empty mind.

Seconds later, the B-door rapidly cracked open, as though someone had deliberately opened it with the intention of causing a loud creaking noise to attract the attention of the teacher in the nearby staff chamber.

Barrie noticed Mable who was hurriedly making her way towards them. She was breathless, panting and gasping for quick, short, breaths. She looked like she had been chased by an enraged mommy dinosaur.

'What's got into you?' Barrie concernedly asked. 'Are you down with wheezing?'

Mable shook her head, trying to inhale every bit of air that was accessible to her.

'You . . . you . . . you won't believe . . . this,' Mable mumbled, taking short breaths in between her words.

'He doesn't believe anything that others say,' Jade said in a pale voice.

'If you are about to say you just finished a ten-mile marathon, I might probably consider believing you,' Barrie amusingly said to his gasping partner, 'providing you show me a dozen empty inhalers.'

'I wasn't talking to you, mean head.' Mable snorted and weakly stretched her hand out at Edy.

'Troniya apologized,' Mable revealed. Her words caught the immediate attention of the uninterested boys, like a powerful magnet drawing a chunk of iron. Mable paused to take a deep breath while Edy and Barrie stared at her, dumbfounded. Jade of course, was only expecting this according to his theoretical findings.

'What?' asked Edy, who rarely looked surprised and bemused at the same time.

'Troniya apologized for her grumpy behaviour last evening.' Mable, who had now considerably recovered from her puffing, continued to astonish the curious listeners, 'And she wants to meet you at the church garden at five today.'

Edy and Barrie turned back at Jade, who now had a flared up nose and a raised eyebrow, a clear sign that showed a 'What did I tell you guys?' look on his face. 'And you both doubted my skilful findings!' Jade angrily said to his astonished friends.

A bright, joy-filled smile fell upon Edy's murky face as he looked back at Mable and signalled his thankfulness to her, which brought an acknowledged nod from her.

As the coffee-break bells went off, grade 10 was back to life. Edy couldn't suppress his desire to look at Troniya.

When he did, she was already looking at him from the corner of her eye. He gestured with a smile, which brought same response from her.

That smile, he thought. *Am I dreaming?* The smile response that he had got was a thousand times more striking than those imaginary smiles that he had been daydreaming about all these days.

Seconds passed like minutes, minutes like hours and hours like days. All that occupied his mind was the fact that Jade was right. *But is he completely right?* Edy thought as he remembered the part where Jade had said about the 'seasoning of the navy-ness' that would ultimately force her to prefer keeping her rank more than anything.

If that's true, then it's gonna be another pessimistic conversation, he unwillingly thought and held on to his best hopes.

At 4.50 p.m., he was in the dormitory, not able to decide on what clothes or which colour he wanted to wear.

Red, he finally thought as he unhooked from the cupboard a red T-shirt that went well with trendy blue trousers.

'Will this do?' he asked himself as he stood in front of the only mirror that was available in the dorm.

At 4.55 p.m., he was still reluctant to get away from the mirror after having tried eight different hairstyles. If you are a guy, I probably don't have to explain the number of attempts we tend to make to look 'stylish'. If you are a girl, then you probably know this better than the guys.

Edy finally managed a hairstyle that was neither too geeky nor too trendy.

At 4.58 p.m., he found himself walking through the openness of the church gardens. He was surprised by the desertedness of the dry landscape. The entire garden floor had a golden-brown grass bed on which the stone slabs were laid that made the pathway to the depths of the garden and led to the church at the extreme end of the school premises. Except for a few buzzing bees and a dozen varieties of rare species of birds, he could not see a single other being.

As he made his way through the lengthy garden path, the frail fragrance of the winter flowers that consisted of lavender, purple and blue crocus filled the air. Far ahead, the sun was fading away. The dimming, glimmering rays painted the sky orange-ish red. The roughness of the harsh winter had eased, and the wind no more knifed through like arrows. A gentle pre-spring breeze had already set in, and it serenely blew at intervals through the enormous deciduous and semi-deciduous trees. The leaves were still shedding, paving way for new ones. A flock of blue jays flew past the old church.

As he neared the church, he felt the bodily changes that he had experienced whenever he was in a situation that involved approaching Troniya. Though the butterflies' hops came back to him, it wasn't as bad as it was the previous evening or as it was in the music room.

At the rear of the church building stood Troniya, waiting.

That can't be true, Edy thought, astounded as he took a far glimpse at her through the straggly leafless branches.

'Red!' he exclaimed softly and a pleased smile fell upon his face. Destiny finally seemed to have favoured its sweet magic on him. He felt as though the unseen forces of the universe had, at last, decided to bring them together.

Or maybe it's just a coincidence! he thought again as his practical mind showed up.

The hard pumping of his heart increased as his every step took him closer towards her until he finally reached the stone slab adjacent to that of Troniya's.

'Umm . . . hi,' Edy greeted her with a gentle smile.

Troniya, who was now looking glad, replied with a gentle 'Hi,' which gave a huge boost to Edy's confidence level.

'I'm really sorry if I kept you waiting,' Edy said.

'No . . . no . . . I just got here,' assured Troniya with a profound smile that half mesmerized Edy. The other half was taken care by her charming voice. Edy smiled back and they walked along the stone path of the rear garden. The orange sun painted the landscape with its dimming radiance as the winter-struck trees kept shedding brownish-yellow leaves.

What a lovely place! Edy thought as he looked far ahead. The fallen leaves danced along the borders of the path as the chilly breeze blew.

Neither of them spoke for a brief minute as they strolled along the golden-brown garden path. Edy was awestruck to no end. He loved the feel that he was experiencing while walking along with his most admired person. The sky dimmed quickly. The gentle wind ruffled through her untied hair as well as the dried yellow leaves on the stone path. Another array of blue jays flew past the high-raised compound wall. The blissfulness of the 'unexplainable with words' feeling that he was going though had far more of an impact on him than anything that he had ever encountered in his entire life.

It was as if one of his favourite imaginary scenarios had come alive. At this point, he had completely forgotten about the pounding heartbeats and the butterflies' quivering.

I'm such an idiot to have chosen to meet her in class when I could have done it in this wonderful place, he thought as he couldn't digest the blissful serenity of the church garden. *What next?* he asked himself.

'So?' Troniya finally broke the silence, still looking at the falling leaves from the deciduous rain trees ahead. 'What is it that you wanted to tell me?' No flute matched the smooth, soothing effect of her tone. She also sounded like she was expecting something very obvious.

'Er . . . um . . . I . . . I . . .' Edy stammered, and in the two-second gap that could squeeze in between his stammering, he was again at war with his inner voice.

Now what do I tell her? Should I use the L word?

Inner Voice: Yes, you should, she's obviously expecting it.

No, that would freak her out, wouldn't it?

Inner Voice: She would want you to be straightforward. Girls don't like guys beating around the bush.

No, not the L word, maybe it's too early as of now.

Inner Voice: You are running out of time.

Doesn't it sound too strong if I use it right now? I might sound desperate.

Inner Voice: This isn't a debate to choose different timings for different words.

There's been nothing between us, not even a frail essence of friendship. She might think I'm moving fast.

Inner Voice: *For God's sake, you have been wanting to tell her this for five months now.*

No, I'm not gonna let her think I'm moving too quick, let me make it smooth and mild.

'Um . . . Well . . . I . . . I might have . . . developed some sort . . . of liking towards you,' Edy said, his heart switching back to hyperactive mode.

Troniya abruptly stopped as if she had run into an invisible wall on the looping pathway. Edy too stopped, taking a fear-filled gulp. At this point, he didn't dare to take a glimpse at her, fearing the kind of possible agitated expression she would have put on.

Both in red, they looked far ahead at the dimming sun. Another flock of blue jays flew past the leafless fire tree on the extreme right corner. A couple of seconds passed. Nothing happened. Edy couldn't suppress his curiosity, which forced him to turn to her. Like a child filled with guilt and after much reluctance, he looked at her. The dim shadow of a thousand tiny twigs fell upon her. The elegance of her beauty had only intensified with the radiance of the reddish-orange glitter. There was absolutely no expression. She bluntly looked ahead, like a statue carved of marble, and that worried Edy to no end.

Without uttering a word, he went back to staring at the setting sun, holding on to his hopes for the best possible reply.

'You don't know much about my dad, do you?' Troniya finally spoke and started to walk again as though the invisible wall had disappeared.

I know, I know he's been with the navy and he's very stern and disciplined, Edy thought but did not reveal it, fearing she might feel she was being stalked. That certainly would be a creepy act according to any girl.

'No.' Edy paused with an extended *o* and looked thoughtful as though recollecting anything that he could about her dad. 'Not really,' he said, 'I haven't had a chance to get to know him.'

'You probably don't want to get to know too much about him,' Troniya said, taking a cursory glance at him.

'No, I really—' Edy couldn't complete his willingness to get to know her dad.

'And you do remember Mr Joseph's warning on the first day, don't you?' Troniya mellifluously interrupted, now looking at him, undistracted.

It didn't take him more than a few milliseconds to recall the scary warning from Mr Joseph. 'It's not like he has to give a written permit.' Edy continued as they both took a different path of the endless loop that took them to a different part of the rear garden, 'Or that he has assigned people to spy on us.'

'We can probably hide from Mr Joseph forever,' Troniya said, going back to looking at the falling leaves, 'but my dad—' She paused and gently shook her head. 'He's not gonna like what I might have to reveal to him.'

Edy put his head down, staring at the dry stone surface filled with dancing golden leaves. His face had turned pale. Troniya was very vigilant to have missed her companion's plight filled face.

So this is it! Edy thought, still staring at every step he put forward. Her words had turned into pungent smoke that choked his ability to speak. He had already predicted that the possibility of a rejection was more than that of acceptance. It was this major thought that had been troubling his restless mind, which in turn had been the reason for many a sleepless night that he had been having for quite some time now.

Just when no hope was left to put him in a confidence loop, Troniya spoke.

'But,' said Troniya, fixing her gaze back at Edy, 'we can always be good friends.' She paused and searched for a more optimistic reaction from her pale partner.

Edy gave an involuntary smile, still looking at the leaf-filled path. It was the smile that had come from deep within, the kind of smile that just shows up at a particular situation, even though you try very hard to suppress it. That's when you know the other person's words meant a lot to you. At once he knew her offer was more than just acceptable. It was, according to his very calculative mind, not a rejection in any way.

Edy looked at her, still having the involuntary smile on him. 'Only if you talk to me more often,' he said, which brought a hearty smile to Troniya.

God, I love her smile, he, who was now deeply looking at her, thought, undistracted by the grunting noise of a heavy vehicle that passed by on the other side of the compound wall. *If only I could freeze time now.*

'Of course we will,' Troniya assured. The rays dimmed, darkening the sky further and the chillness of the air dropped drastically.

They walked back through the garden in silence. Being in her company was such a wonderful feeling that he felt all the worldly treasures and riches faded away into nothingness, and though he was blissfully contented at what he had gotten, a small part in him knew he hadn't really gotten what he essentially wanted.

Everybody knows how that feels. You know how that feels, don't you? It's like getting a 45 on 50, though you were expecting a 48 on 50. No, not 49 on 50. You aren't Troniya, are you?

*   *   *   *   *   *

Absorption in Bliss

All those scenarios that we make up in our heads when we start to like someone—and we tend to make an awful lot of almost impossible scenarios—have practically no end. The fantasized scenario gets all the more fantastic especially when the situation is favourable. We dream and dream about all the momentous scenarios that involve deserted, peaceful places—the number one on the list being 'lost on a remote island'. Of course not alone, but with the only person we ever wanted to be lost on a remote island with.

What's ironic is that we also tend to create all the goodies that we require to survive on the remote island. Availability of fire, food, and shelter is a definite must in order to not cause much trouble to the survival while we are spending a great deal of time to try and impress our partner. We also go on to the luxuries that might include a abandoned leak-proof wooden house filled with stock of processed edibles, fishing nets, hunting tools, and whatnot. On the outside would be an abandoned but perfectly usable boat, varieties of edible fauna and flora, and lots of coconut trees around. Of course all this is set in a beautiful, breathtaking background of the setting sun. The delicious, juicy fried fish that we manage to cook on an improvised earthen grill is something that cannot be missed either.

And statistically speaking, 90 per cent of us end up in a daydream even without our knowledge. Those thoughts are infinite. We get lost so deeply that we forget the minor things like our surroundings, the time of the day, and the condition of the surroundings, among various other fundamentals.

Miss Andrella had already finished half of the chapter 'The Vigilante of Venickor' when she was outraged to notice, for the fourth time in a row, a dreaming Edy who had become totally oblivious of her lecture. It was a hi-fi dream, the one in which no amount of distractions or scary staring could cause even the slightest effect on the victim.

'Edy,' Miss Andrella finally called out after she had lost all hopes of getting him back to listening to her with her scary stare. All forty-seven pairs of curious eyes turned towards Edy, who was now looking at Miss Andrella, transfixed. 'What page are we on?' Miss Andrella calmly asked. Edy was petrified and, even more, embarrassed for being in the spotlight for the wrong reason. But thanks to his trustable friend who, like any trustable friend, would go to any extent to save him from a potential hazardous situation, even if that meant putting himself at great risk of being caught for helping Edy. Barrie stealthily nudged Edy, who took a very quick, almost instantaneous, sneaky look at his neighbour's open text that showed the tiny numbers at the bottom of the page.

'One twenty-eight,' he answered doubtfully.

Miss Andrella did not question him further but gave a serious 'I see what you did there' look before going back to lecturing.

Ugh, that was some serious lucky escape, Edy thought as the forty-seven pairs of eyes went back to following Miss Andrella's movements.

'Stop dreaming,' Barrie whispered, not taking his eyes off the lecturer.

I'm trying, Edy thought, which didn't help him in any way. He had met Troniya a couple of times over the week under closed eye—a phrase which here means 'met secretively to avoid any unnecessary rumours spreading in grade 10' as they had decided back at the church garden. And the thought that he was to meet her that evening was what had sparked the hi-fi daydream.

The big evening did come sooner than he had expected. As Edy waited back in class, his heart's pounding didn't switch to hyperactive mode anymore. It was their fourth meeting after they had agreed to be good friends. The keeping count of the meetings was an indispensable part of Edy's routine now. This was the count that marked his standards for the basis of making each day count.

The senior corridor was quiet again. Moments later, Troniya was seen entering the B-corridor.

Wow, Edy thought as he took a glimpse at her from a distance, *a new hairstyle.* Her footsteps drew closer until finally Edy could clearly see the arduously done hair.

'I love what you have done to your hair,' he complimented Troniya as she entered through the B-door, half shutting it as she stepped in.

'Thank you,' Troniya said with a smile that looked more like a blush to Edy.

'I'm hoping today is a special day for you,' Edy said leaning on Wenda Alexander's desk as Troniya stood opposite to him.

'What makes you think that?' she questioned, running her fingers through the curly tips of her hair.

'Your new hairstyle,' Edy said, quickly scrutinizing every inch of the painstakingly done hair, 'it must have taken an awful lot of time to have it done.'

'Stop with your detective scanning already,' pleaded Troniya, who by now had known how minutely Edy observed the world around him.

'So, is it your birthday?' Edy asked.

'No,' Troniya said, 'if it was, then I would have been called onstage in the assembly today.'

'I can't think of any other reason for the rigorously done hair,' Edy admitted, still scanning every minute detail of the work done.

'Birthdays aren't the only special occasions,' Troniya said, looking away from Edy.

'Christmas passed two weeks ago,' Edy said, looking up thoughtfully, 'and I can't think of any other festive event that might happen anytime soon.'

'I didn't mean about the festivals.'

'Okay,' Edy said with a long *kay*, 'then?'

'Um . . . well,' Troniya began, now avoiding eye contact with her companion, 'meeting someone important might also be considered as a special occasion.'

What? Edy instantaneously thought. *Did I just hear what I just heard? And why is her smile looking more like a blush?*

Edy was baffled to no end as he tried to decode her confusing words which again started a ten-second-long battle with his inner voice.

Does that mean she likes me, which is why she considers me to be important?

Inner Voice: Of course, that's the obvious explanation.

Or is she playing around just to keep me in the guessing loop?

Inner Voice: Well, she's blushing, there's your signal.

Girls always blush when they say things to confuse others.

Inner Voice: This one doesn't look like it's put on to confuse you.

Damn, if only I could read her mind.

'I'm hoping you are not meeting anyone else later in the evening,' Edy said with an exaggerated understanding.

Troniya dimly shook her head and continued curling her black, shiny hair.

Momentary silence fell. Edy continued saving clear mental images of her as her hair looked like a diamond crown on a princess, which made her beauty all the more elegant.

'So,' Troniya spoke, now looking at him with a dimmed smile, 'how's your preparation going for the end-of-term?'

'Um . . . er . . . I . . .' Edy struggled to reveal the truth. 'Well, I'm dealing with a more important, life-concerning matter right now, so preparations aren't really on top of the list as of now.'

Troniya's smile, which dimmed further, gave way to a more serious-looking stare. She wasn't curling her curly ends anymore. Her pretty eyes shined like black beetles on a hot sunny afternoon.

She definitely doesn't like my attitude towards the upcoming exams, Edy thought as he observed the expressional changes.

'You do know this is our first turning point in our lives,' Troniya reminded him seriously.

'What?' Edy instantaneously interrupted, mystified.

'I meant the exams. You do realize this is *your* first turning point in *your* academic career?' Troniya elaborated her concern more clearly.

'Oh . . . that . . . I know,' said Edy with a dull tone, looking at the scribbled blackboard. 'I'm trying, but it's just this new feeling that I have absolutely no control of, it's . . . it's like an invisible magnet.' Edy continued, switching his gaze to different parts of the blackboard, 'I'm being drawn towards someone—I mean, something.' Edy quickly substituted the word.

Troniya's blush rushed back almost instantly. This time it was more vividly intense than earlier. She started with the curls again, now looking at the half-opened B-door.

'Your new hairstyle does really suit you,' Edy said as he gawped at her.

'Thank you,' Troniya blushingly said, still looking through the half opened B-door.

Edy couldn't wait to tell his best buddies, Barrie and Jade, what had happened back in class that evening. Jade was informed first though, as Edy wanted to have

Troniya's mysterious words and confusing expressions decoded and analyzed.

And after a detailed analysis of the scene later that evening, Jade had reached a glorious conclusion: 'She definitely has the pre-feel embedded in her, but she might still be oblivious to it, all you have to do is give it some more time.'

Edy's glooming heart jumped up and down on listening to Jade's favourable conclusion. His imaginary confetti had begun to rain all over him.

'Thank goodness I didn't give her the rose today,' Edy said with a strong relief.

'Rose?' Jade and Barrie asked, baffled.

'Yes,' Edy revealed, 'I had taken a yellow rose today, to make our friendship bond stronger.'

'Right, yellow for friendship,' Jade interrupted.

'But now,' Edy continued with a deep contentment, 'seems like yellow isn't the right colour after all.'

'A rose wasted, then,' Barrie sighed.

'No, I'm not gonna throw it.'

'It isn't exactly an artificial one, is it?'

'No.'

'So it's gonna die and lose its colour sooner than it was supposed to,' Barrie, a nature lover, sighed.

'I won't let that happen.' Edy continued, 'All these tiny things will be the best memories that I'm gonna share with her someday in the distant future.'

'Please feel free to exclude me if you are planning on stealing the life-preserving chemical from the chemistry lab for its preservation,' Barrie said as he remembered what had happened to him when he had tried to steal the 'wonder fire chemical' the previous year.

'That's a great idea,' Jade said, snapping his fingers. 'That will preserve the rose if we can manage to get some.'

'It's practically been impossible to steal from the chemistry lab since the installation of CCTVs in all the science labs,' Barrie pointed out.

'Guys, please,' Edy interrupted the debaters. 'I know of another method,' Edy said, sounding like a scientist who had a major breakthrough in his research.

'I don't see any other possible way to do so,' Barrie admitted. Jade nodded in agreement.

Edy hazily smiled with an 'I know just the right trick' look.

*　　*　　*　　*　　*　　*

The following Sunday morning at breakfast, Edy did notice Troniya smiling at him. He neither had to peep through the many blocking heads nor had to nudge Barrie to move to the right as Troniya had positioned herself in the sweet spot that provided a clear view.

It wasn't just a plain smile that they had exchanged. It was the special smile, the one that you give to someone in order to signal that you have acknowledged their smile with a smile that matched the intensity of the other's smile.

That morning as they both exchanged their special smiles, Edy was absorbed in bliss. Her smile radiated vibrations of purity and love that he could feel at this very first stage. A bottomless feeling of profound fulfilment emanated in him that provided a robust threshold, preventing any negativity from deterring his unwavering thoughts and decisions concerning her. Her smile also bestowed him with inner tranquillity, a divine sense of understanding the world around him, contentment, and ability to judge matters fervently.

His boundless shyness and fear detached, to be replaced with confidence and willpower that matched the energy of undetonated dynamite. His mind was now unalterably fixed on her and his endless thoughts faded away into silence as he looked deeper into her graceful eyes.

That evening, a January Sunday, was the day when Edy finally decided to move ahead with his plans. As he waited back in class, he could sense things were going just as he wanted them to—accordingly, smoothly, and without any obstacles at all.

Life can't get better, Edy thought as he, stealthily peeked into the B-corridor through the half opened B-door. The corridor was as calm as it could get. A minute later, he could see Troniya entering the corridor.

Another new hairstyle, Edy said to himself as he opened the door further to sneak a quick look, *even better than the previous one.*

He stood still as Troniya walked closer, until finally she noticed him blocking the doorway. 'I must admit, your new hairstyle is absolutely stunning, you look very pretty,' Edy finally complimented her, which he had been holding back for quite some time now, 'like the Princess of Penensillwielle.'

'I wasn't yesterday?' Troniya asked, leaning against one of the supporting pillars of the B-corridor.

'You were, you are, and you will always be,' Edy said, which brought a soft, slow-motion blushing smile on Troniya, after which she started with the curling soon after.

'I can only assume you are trying to impress someone with all the new styles,' Edy said. The bluishness remained intact as she looked away from him.

'Maybe,' Troniya said, turning towards the lengthy, empty, noiseless B-corridor.

'You really don't have to do it with such arduous work of doing your hair,' Edy paused for a while, to intake with his eyes, the elegance of her boundless charm that was radiating from her unsurpassable beauty. . 'A simple smile would do the trick.'

Troniya's continued blushing and curling her smooth, shiny, straightened hair that no longer had the curls at the ends. Her smile attracted him towards her with biting intensity.

How I wish this moment could freeze in time forever, he wishfully thought as his super consciousness had been taken over by semi-consciousness as he got lost gazing at the mixture of beauty, serenity, and everlasting waves of positive vibrations emanating from her blush. By now he had realized how inordinately he was fond of her.

'So,' Troniya spoke, fixing her gaze at his gazing eyes, 'how are things going with you?'

'With you around, there's nothing that can ever go wrong,' Edy admitted that sounded more like a flirty statement than a complimentary one.

Troniya shook her head dimly and with a 'you have gone crazy' look.

'I really love what you have done to your hair.' Edy admired her with much esteem, 'You look exceptionally gorgeous.'

Troniya's curling was intensified right after the brief beauty admiration statement.

'Tell me something that you haven't already told me,' Troniya said taking a quick but deep look at her companion.

What does she mean by that? Edy thought, confused by her words, like always.

Inner Voice: There, that's your signal to go ahead with the proposal.

Edy's unpredictable inner voice sprang up all of a sudden.

No, that can't be it. It was just a conversation statement, with no hidden messages.

Inner Voice: Definitely with a hidden message, she wants you to step up with the proposal, in the proper manner, with the L word.

I wish Jade was here for the analysis.

Inner Voice: I'm a better analyzer. You are about to miss the only opportunity that you have got.

No, she denied earlier.

Inner Voice: That doesn't mean she'll remain with denial forever. Open your heart, this is the right moment, let her know how you feel about her. *Do it!*

'I want to, but you might not like it,' Edy said, searching Troniya's face for an expression other than her constant blush.

'You can always give it a try,' Troniya said, looking back into the corridor.

Inner Voice: You are an idiot!

'I don't know,' Edy said ignoring his inner voice's offensive remark. 'I mean, clearly you didn't approve it earlier . . . Um . . . so . . . you . . . might . . . not.' Troniya's smile dimmed.

Inner Voice: *What* have you done? You are ruining it all.

'Honestly, I'm too scared to tell it to you openly,' Edy admitted, dragging his head low.

Inner Voice: Just tell her the damn sentence with the L word.

The voice had turned aggressive and loud.

'You could always write it down,' Troniya suggested, taking another cursory look at his floor- facing face.

She's definitely expecting the L word, Edy confidently thought.

'You're right,' he said with a bold smile, 'I can do that.' And he rushed back to his desk and quickly returned with an empty sheet and a blue ballpoint pen.

As Edy held the empty sheet against the metal B-door, he knew exactly what he wanted to write and in which language. To avoid any serious consequences should the sheet happen to fall in the wrong hands like those of the authorities, he used the students' secret language that was famously popular among the pupils of MPS.

Edy wrote: J GPUB ZPV WMPQJZF!

Troniya quickly decoded the message at a speed that stunned Edy and wrote in reply: J HQPT WKFW FGMBFCZ

Edy: EVW J KFUBQ'W WPGC ZPV ZBW

Troniya: J HQPT WKFW WPP

Edy: XP?

Troniya: XP?

Edy: FQZ WKPVLKWX PQ WKFW?

Troniya: QPOB, QPW MBFGGZ

Edy: ZPV RVXW KFUB XPRBWKJQL WP XFZ WP WKFW

Troniya: FDWVFGGZ J CP

Edy: TPVGC GPUB WP HQPT JW

Troniya: LPPC WKJQLX DPRB WP WKPXB TKP TFJW!

Both Edy and Troniya exchanged a brief smile as Edy decoded the last message.

This is it, Edy thought. *She's definitely not just a friend anymore.*

'And you wanted Jade to be here to interpret her obvious words and expressions,' his inner voice shot back at him.

Well, now I'm sure about this, he placidly replied to his arrogant inner voice.

* * * * * *

A Touch of Love

*E*ver wondered how a boon of superhuman power might save you from all the ill things that might occur in your life? Hypothetically, if you were to choose one special superhuman power, what would it be? Well, I would opt for the 'universal hearing' super power. With that, I would be able to hear anything I wish to hear, with the snap of my finger. For example, I would be able to hear all the jealous talks that might happen when I'm not around. Or if at all my enemies are planning a surprise attack on me while I'm sleeping. Or all the negative comments that my boss might give to the department head. Isn't it wonderful to hear any remote conversation that involves your name?

Sadly our universe isn't that parallel universe that grants us super human boons. Consequently, like you and me, Edy too didn't exactly have the powers to listen to the obnoxious conversation that happened right after the first hour.

Miss Andrella headed back to the staff chambers, angrily. Her irritated thoughts kept pestering her to take severe actions against a particular student, possibly to relieve her from the dire consequences of not reporting a potential misconduct of a student.

As Miss Andrella reached the coffee vending machine, she dumped the files and grade 10 English text on the adjacent table. Her conspicuous actions did catch the attention of Mr Hal and Miss Adeline, who were sipping their cups of coffee while having a chattering conversation.

'What's wrong, Miss Andrella?' Mr Hal asked with high curiosity, so was his concern.

Miss Andrella sighed as she filled the cup with an unusually strong latte. Miss Adeline took a detailed look at the grade 10 text that had been dumped next to the coffee vending machine. 'Grade 10?' Miss Adeline asked, 'Something's wrong in grade 10, Miss Andrella?'

'I strongly hope it isn't anything about the class representative,' said Mr Hal, who had now stopped sipping his cup of hot beverage.

'Of course it is.' Miss Andrella snorted, looking at Mr Hal and Miss Adeline alternately throughout her sentence. 'Haven't you both had any trouble with him lately?'

'Well, his behaviour hasn't exactly been what it used to be,' Mr Hal admitted. 'That I am very sure of.'

'I thought I was the only facing this nonsense behaviour of his!' Miss Adeline joined in, not sipping her coffee anymore.

'I was under the same assumption as well,' Mr Hal said, looking at his seated colleague, 'at least until now.'

'Are you saying that he's been dreaming in your classes too?' Miss Andrella asked with a more concerned voice, shocked at the teachers' concerns.

Both the seated faculty members nodded, holding their cups motionless.

'I wonder what's got into him lately,' Miss Andrella whined, carefully placing her un-sipped strong latte down on the table.

'Just the other day, I was lecturing on Java, a new and complicated computer language,' Mr Hal explained, 'and he was gleefully staring at the wall ahead, as though he were watching a mockumentary.'

'Exactly,' Miss Adeline agreed.

'Shouldn't we be escalating this to the principal?' Miss Andrella asked.

'I was thinking the same,' Mr Hal said.

'The sooner the better,' Miss Adeline suggested eagerly, after which the three teachers headed towards the Chambers of Principal Authority.

'Excuse me, sir, may we come in?' Mr Hal interrupted the usually very busy principal.

'Yes, please,' Mr Joseph permitted them, peeping from under his spectacles. The door was opened further and in walked Mr Hal, Miss Andrella, and Miss Adeline. 'What's the matter with you three?'

'We are here to express our concerns on a student who has been off the track lately.' Mr Hal said, as the three each occupied a chair.

'Name the student and I will take a severe action against him or her,' Mr Joseph said, shuffling the documents on his table.

'Edy Ravenden, sir,' Miss Andrella revealed.

'What?' Mr Joseph asked, shocked, while the three angry complainers nodded in agreement.

'Indeed, sir, Edy of grade—'

'Are you sure of who are complaining against?' Mr Joseph interrupted Mr Hal.

'More than just sure, sir,' Miss Adeline said, while the other two looked exceedingly confident.

Mr Joseph sat still, transfixed and looking at the three enraged complainers. 'There must be something fishy going on, then.' Mr Joseph continued, dropping the documents from his hands, 'How can a primary class representative misbehave all of a sudden?'

'Of course, sir, he was a very scholarly student of grade 10 until a few days ago,' Mr Hal said regretfully, 'but now he isn't what he used to be.'

'He's not following our lectures anymore,' Miss Andrella desperately lodged the complaint. 'He's distracted to a great extent.'

Mr Joseph thought for a moment as the three infuriated teachers waited for a reply. 'I will look into this matter right away.' Mr Joseph assured them sternly.

'Thank you for your cooperation, sir, your involvement will definitely have a great impact on him.' Mr Hal thanked the principal, and the three complainers left the chamber.

Mr Joseph immediately sent for Edy. Moments later, the personal assistant returned with the accused.

'Excuse me, sir, may I come in?' Edy gladly requested, not knowing why he had been called upon to the Chambers of Principal Authority.

'Come in,' Mr Joseph said and brought his busy work to an abrupt halt.

'So, Edy, is everything fine with you?' Mr Joseph asked with an intense stern look.

'Of course, sir,' Edy answered in a softer tone than earlier.

'If it was, then I wouldn't have had not one but three teachers coming in earlier today with severe complaints against you.'

Edy's cheeks turned red; his ears warmed up instantly.

'Sir?' Edy asked as his smile sank down.

'You do know what's going on with you.' Mr Joseph started to express his concern, 'You are the primary class representative, and these aren't the sorts of comments that I should be receiving from the faculty members.'

Edy put his head down, staring at the shiny, black reflective floor. 'I'm sorry, sir,' he faintly said.

'It isn't about being sorry, it's about keeping your position high above the ground.' Mr Joseph briefly paused. 'Are you being influenced by the bad guys of the class?' Mr Joseph suspiciously asked.

'No, sir, I'm not.'

'Anyone would say that but how can I believe?' Mr Joseph continued, 'I know the amount of stress that grade 10 and grade 12 students are going through right now. It's definitely taking a toll on the pressure levels of the students, given that these are the two most important year of their academic careers.'

Edy listened seriously, looking at Mr Joseph with utmost attentiveness.

'To counter that stress, involve yourself in non-academic work, have a hobby. It isn't a compulsory one though, it's just a spare time activity to keep your mind relaxed.'

Edy nodded as he kept looking at Mr Joseph to signal to him that he took the latter's words seriously.

'Some people like to paint, while others like to admire paintings. Some like to play musical instruments, while others simply listen to them. Some like to write stories, while others like to read them,' Mr Joseph continued, giving a long lecture which was totally unrelated to Edy's actual situation. 'Be the first kind, you will be both eminent and acknowledged. Or be the second kind, you will be distinguished from those who do not have hobbies at all.'

Edy nodded at the end of each sentence, waiting for the boring lecture to end.

'Choose hobbies that are entirely different from the typical work to help you relax better. The more unusual the hobby, the more interesting it gets.'

'I got it, sir,' Edy willingly assured him. 'I will do my best to keep up the dignity of a class representative and uphold the badge of office.'

Mr Joseph gave one last look to see if Edy was confident enough of what he had said. 'All I want is an assurance that there won't be any further complaints against you, by any of the faculty members,' Mr Joseph said sternly, 'failing which, I will be forced to take severe action.'

'I promise you, sir,' Edy doubtfully assured him, 'there won't be any.'

'You can go now,' Mr Joseph said and quickly resumed his paperwork.

Edy walked out of the chamber, irately. He well knew Miss Andrella was one of the three complainers, but he wondered who the other two were. His juvenile blood boiled as he couldn't believe he had just been in the Chambers of Principal Authority for the wrong reason.

All that anger that had been gathering in his spine vanished in an instant as he entered the class. Troniya was already looking at him with a concerned 'Why were you called by Joseph's assistant?' look. Edy pointed at his metal badge and signalled that he was called upon official duty and gave an 'Everything's just fine' smile. Troniya's troubled smile turned to a more pleasant one on the assurance that she had just received. The thought that he was to meet her that evening stomped away all his worries in the blink of an eye.

As he waited back in class on the same evening, he dreamt of all those myriad of splendid days he wanted to spend with her. Each second that he was spending in her company was becoming an invaluable treasure to him.

The B-door creaked open, and Edy was still lost in his favourably plotted imaginary world. He was at a standstill even as Troniya approached him. Finally, she stood next to the teacher's table, waiting for him to say something.

Edy only stood like a statue, looking at his charming companion and her mesmerizing ocean-like eyes. His mind was already half blank, with the other half dealing with how to assimilate such immense beauty. Troniya patiently waited for him to get out of his dreaming moment as she leaned on the teacher's table.

'I'm already here,' Troniya said, deeply looking into his lost eyes, 'in case you didn't notice.'

'Oh damn!' Edy thought and faintly twitched. 'Uh . . . I'm sorry,' Edy spoke, smiling weirdly, 'I was . . . um . . . I was recollecting the lectures of today's classes,' Edy said, which Troniya knew wasn't true. . 'You know . . . being serious . . . about the upcoming end-term exams.'

'Really?' Troniya asked with a mild frown along with a smile.

'Yup.' Edy continued looking at the blackboard ahead. 'I'm seriously serious about the seriousness that one should have towards life's goals.'

'Is that why you were caught dreaming in Miss Andrella's class?'

'No . . . I mean . . . um . . . yes.' Edy's reluctant mumbling brought the blushing smile back on Troniya's ever-captivating face.

Thank God! Edy thought, relieved. *I thought she was gonna get serious on this.*

'But anyway, you are quite smart,' Troniya let out her first ever compliment, 'academically clever, so it won't really be a hitch for you to score good marks.'

'Not as smart as you,' Edy complimented her in return. 'You are like, the smartest of all the smart people that I have ever known.'

'Really?' Troniya asked with the frowning back on.

'Of course, that's something very unquestionable,' Edy said, recollecting the first test score. 'I mean . . . 49 on 50 in the first ever class test—that was undeniably some serious score.'

'You remember my first test score?' Troniya asked, flabbergasted. Her reply came at the speed of a lightning bolt.

Damn it, now she'll think I have been stalking her from the beginning, Edy thought.

'Who doesn't?' Edy's quick-witted brain hatched a convincing explanation. 'Everyone in grade 10 remembers a practically impossible score, 49 on 50.' Edy continued praising his companion with a lot of enthusiasm in his voice. 'That's something that cannot be missed. I have never come across that score ever, not in Miss Andrella's paper, not in any other teacher's paper.'

'You are kidding, right?'

Edy sternly shook his head.

'Well, thank you for the compliment,' she gracefully said, 'I guess everyone has their own talent, and is smart in their own ways, like you.'

'Me?' Edy asked with an expression that matched an innocent victim who had been deliberately charged with a mystery robbery.

'Yes, you wrote that poem, I remember!' Troniya cheerfully said, 'It was one among the top eight, wasn't it?'

'Yes, it was!'

'That's some serious creativity, I must admit.'

'You like reading poems?'

'I would prefer them over any other literature works.'

'I'm so glad,' Edy said, feeling like an overnight-famous celebrity. 'So did you like mine?'

'The best among those selected eight,' Troniya declared.

Wow, Edy thought as he put on his version of a proud face.

'Well, thank you,' he delightedly said, 'then I'm gonna write a thousand poems for you.'

'I would love to read them!' Troniya said, showing a lot of eagerness.

A minute of silence followed, Edy slowly losing his sense as he slipped back into his dreamy world.

'So what's your future plan?' Troniya asked, interrupting Edy's brief daydream.

'Um . . . I haven't really decided yet, what's yours?'

'It really depends on my dad's work transfers,' Troniya honestly replied.

'Oh, that's awful,' Edy said with a brief sigh.

'I know,' Troniya said. 'Shifting to a new place is such a straining job.'

'I hope everything goes well.'

'But anyway, you will definitely get into a good college, I'm sure.'

'We, you mean,' Edy said.

'Yes, I as well, hopefully,' Troniya smilingly said.

'You probably hate it here,' Edy continued, leaning on row 3, desk 1. 'You know . . . first year at a boarding school, away from your family.'

'How do you know all this stuff?' Troniya asked, putting on her suspicious-confused frown.

'I mean . . . the girls told me.'

'Mable?'

'Um . . . yup . . . Mable, Celia, and probably a few guys.'

'Bonn!' Troniya exclaimed.

'Um . . . yeah . . . like Bonn.'

'He was a good friend of mine until one day he stopped talking of a sudden,' Troniya said, looking thoughtful. 'I wonder what happened.'

Damn, that was by my influence, Edy thought guiltily, *I shouldn't have teased him to that extent.*

'He's a weirdo,' Edy said. 'Don't worry about him.'

'I thought so,' Troniya amusingly said, 'but definitely not as weird as Ivan.'

Edy's inner rage-filled jealousy sprang up to his head.

'You talk to him a lot?' he worriedly enquired.

'I don't,' Troniya disclosed what was, until now, unknown to Edy, 'but he always does. I can't just sit like a deaf person, so I'm forced to talk.'

Ivan, you're so dead, Edy thought, clenching his teeth hard.

'I only hope he isn't troubling you' Edy doubtfully said.

'No, he isn't troubling, but he gets annoying sometimes,' Troniya said and looked at her pink-strapped watch.

'It's fifty past five,' Troniya read out from her white-dialled wristwatch.

'Should we disperse?' Edy unwillingly asked.

Troniya dimly nodded.

'Thursday? Same time? Same place?' Edy asked.

'Thursday sounds good,' Troniya said, smiling cheerfully.

What next? Edy thought, *Should I move ahead with the plan or not?*

Undeniably it's a yes, his inner voice sprang up from nowhere.

Isn't it too early? Maybe I should wait until our next meeting.

It's never too early to start any good move, his inner voice encouraged.

Yeah, what the hell, he thought and stretched out his hand.

'Sure, until Thursday then!'

Will she? Will she not? Will she? Will she not? Will she? Will she not? Edy plucked the uncountable petals from his imaginary flower.

She will, his inner voice guaranteed.

No, she won't, he insisted, looking at her with a mild smile. This was his first strong move that he had ever made to get close to her.

She won't take it, Edy thought, his shivery, warm hand still stretched out like the branch of a decorated Christmas tree.

For three lengthy seconds, Troniya looked preoccupied, alternating her gaze at him and his hand, thinking how she wanted to react until finally she decided what was favourable for Edy.

She stretched her hand out and reached Edy's lukewarm palm.

'Until Thursday,' she said, mildly shaking hands with him.

No. If you are thinking there has been a printing error, the answer is no. Those pages were intentionally left blank, to give you an actual glimpse of what was going through Edy's mind for the next ten seconds.

As Edy felt her flowery soft hand, he hadn't had an inkling of a clue as to how his body and mind would react, until after a few seconds after the handshake; he realized his senses were all gone on a short 'disappearance tour'.

Troniya's words did not exactly register in his mind. All he saw was the blurry lip movement. He stood there like a life-size statue carved out of wood. His eyelids didn't blink anymore; his hand shivered no more and thoughts passed in emptiness.

Troniya gradually stepped out of the B-door, turned towards her 'lost in nothingness' partner and gave a confused blushing smile.

Edy's senses were restored to their original working capacity after about a minute as he retracted his hand, which he felt no longer belonged to his body.

As he briefly looked at his palm, a feeling of absoluteness ran from his palm to the rest of his body. *I'm never letting her go off my life, no matter what,* he thought, and gently closed his fist.

The invisible vibrations of the 'don't know how to explain' feeling that he had had because of the handshake remained intact for an unbelievably long time. At regular intervals, he kept looking at his palm and that brought about an involuntary smile on him.

A confused Barrie finally brought out his curiousness. 'What's with the hand?' he asked after having noticed Edy's strange behaviour later that evening

Edy mutely shook his head and his smile broadened.

'Ah . . . the handshake effect, isn't it?' Barrie suspiciously asked, which brought a nodding action from his companion.

'I thought so,' Barrie said, 'I hope you don't get lost too much in your dreamy world and forget about the upcoming important events.'

'What important events?' Edy asked, still looking at his hand.

'Gifts!'

'Gifts?' Edy asked, now looking at Barrie, 'What gifts?'

'The fourteenth of February, Valentine's Day,' Barrie reminded.

'Right,' Edy said with a deep realization. 'How on earth am I supposed to buy her gifts?'

'We do have a parents–teachers meeting this Saturday,' Barrie reminded.

'The outing.'

'That's our only chance.'

Edy knew exactly what he wanted to do the following Saturday afternoon, in the short three-hour outing time that he was going to have.

*   *   *   *   *   *

Undelivered Valentine's Gifts

*S*oon enough, the much awaited Saturday arrived and the parents–teachers meeting lasted until half past one. Though Edy didn't, in particular, receive the usually positive comments on his performance from the senior teacher, he didn't seem to be bothered by what they had to say, unlike his mom and dad. They were in for a bad time when they stepped into Miss Andrella's cubicle.

On the pretext of personal shopping, Edy separated from his parents on the busy Jev Dur Ras shopping street, and after a quick search on the lengthy road, he found the right shop that he wanted to go to. The huge building had a huge bright red board with the words 'Arch's—The Best Gift Shop' emblazoned in bright white light.

As Edy set foot in Arch's, he was surrounded by a swarming, excited mob. The colossal store was filled with abundant gift items. Not able to decide what gift he wanted to buy, Edy sprang a scanning look at the million items that were neatly arranged in an unambiguous order.

As he walked ahead, there were several bright-lit aisles that had multiple layers with different-sized items that were kept for sale. On the left aisle, there were huge multicoloured bears, talking bears and walking bears, brilliant pieces of abstract artwork, dancing heart-shaped helium balloons, fabricated photo frames of different sizes, shapes, and colours, green-gold jewellery, glowing showpieces, glittering greeting cards that were huge enough to wrap a small TV.

On the right aisle, there were bright blue bouquets, metallic make-up sets, sparkling metal stars, fabric flowers of all possible varieties that were elegantly arranged in vibrant vases, chunky aromatic cylindrical candles ornamented with shiny silver stars, antique ashtrays, Scrabble boards and other board games stuffed in straight lines, marvellous wall hangings and oil paintings, colourful woollen scarves, festooned wall clocks, painted pen holders, and stringed puppet dolls.

On the far corner aisle, there were glossy coffee cups, see-through perfume bottles that were studded with colourful pearls, lustrous night lamps, classy crystal clocks, flickering finger rings, and several collections of expensive wine bottles, under which there were plain wine glasses. In the edibles section, there were delicious chocolates, cakes and cookies, palatable pastries with several fruity flavours, packed heart-shaped dark chocolates, and heart-shaped lollipops. As Edy moved ahead to the furthermost right corner, he came across a small shelf that contained the smallest gifts available in the store.

'Wow,' Edy faintly exclaimed in enthrallment as he peeped through the protective glass door. He was impressed as he minutely observed how endearing those gifts were. After carefully examining all the tiny items on the shelf, he selected two that he wished to gift to his lady love. The fragility of the items on the glass shelf made him move his steady fingers all the more gently so as to make sure he didn't damage the neighbouring delicate objects. With great fondness, he picked up the two items and dotingly held on to them.

The first one was a small square-shaped book (smaller than his palm) which contained about twenty-five pages of love quotes. On every adjacent page was a flowery depiction of the quote's meaning. The second was a small, red, black, and white coloured coffee cup that was heart shaped from the top and the words 'Loving Is More Fulfilling Than Being Loved' inscribed on one of its sides.

Both the gifts were perfectly designed and selected for an ideal Valentine's Day. As Edy showed off his own Valentine's gifts, Barrie was surprised. 'Those are some enviable gifts for a first timer,' Barrie musingly commented as he took a closer look at the two little objects.

'Thanks, Barrie,' Edy replied. 'Plus I had to sneak them in without my mom and dad knowing it.'

Barrie heartily giggled and said, 'Welcome to the world of sneaking, mate, from now on that's gonna be a major part of your life.'

The Tenth Meet
Friday, 9 February 2007

Edy and Troniya were back in class as according to their meeting plan. *Why is she not so happy today?* was the first thought that went through Edy's worried mind as he noticed the not-so-cheerful expression on Troniya's face that evening.

What could possibly be the reason? Edy thought as they chattered away as usual, but without the blushing smiles on either of their faces.

Should I ask her what's troubling her? Edy asked himself, halfway through their thirty-minute chat.

'Ask her, go ahead,' his inner voice sprang up from nowhere.

No, maybe she doesn't want to share it with me, Edy replied.

'You can always try asking!' the inner voice urged him.

If she wanted me to know, she would have told me long ago, he resisted.

'Aren't you gonna ask what's troubling her?' the inner voice shouted loud inside.

'So what's troubling you?' Edy finally asked after he had gathered the required amount of courage.

'Sorry?' Troniya said, still leaning against the teacher's table.

'Isn't something troubling you?' Edy suspiciously asked.

'No,' Troniya said, sternly shaking her head, at the same time putting on an 'Everything is fine' smiley expression.

Okay, she definitely doesn't want me to know, no more forcing, Edy stringently thought.

'You might want to lose your detective adroitness of others' expressions,' Troniya suggested, still smiling.

'Really? Why?'

'Might not always be comfortable for others.'

'Are *you* feeling uncomfortable about it?'

'No, no . . . not at all,' Troniya instantly replied. 'Maybe for your rivals.'

'My rivals?' Edy was taken aback. 'I don't have any,' he insisted.

'I heard about Bryan's story,' Troniya revealed.

I'm so dead, Edy fearfully thought. *How did she get to know that?*

'It was just a one-time quarrel,' he honestly admitted, 'plus he deserved it.'

Troniya's smile faded away as she heard Edy.

Okay she's definitely the pro-non-violence kind, he at once thought.

'But I promised myself not to indulge in any fights from then on,' Edy said, which brought a slim but profound smile on Troniya.

A dull minute passed in silence. Edy kept thinking hard how on earth she got to know about the 'Bryan beaten in bathroom' story.

'Evidently someone's been trying hard to find out my past details,' Edy said, avoiding all visual contact with his partner.

'What makes you think that?' Troniya asked.

'You surely got to know about the fight which, until now, I thought was a much-guarded top secret.'

'That wasn't deliberately found out,' Troniya said.

Edy put on a 'Then how did you know?' look.

'I have my sources and there's a lot that goes on in the girls' dormitory.'

'Really?'

'Yup, all the biggest secrets of MPS are matters of regular gossip in there,' Troniya swiftly revealed, 'both rumours and facts.'

'Wow,' Edy exclaimed, 'too many secret revealers, then.'

'Way too many,' Troniya said and revealed some of those that she had heard.

They laughed over the secretive jokes that Troniya had recently heard from the gossipers group.

How do I convey to her my plans for the fourteenth? Edy thought as he laughed through the last rumour that Troniya had revealed.

'So what are you doing on the fourteenth?' Edy asked, trying to make it sound nothing more than a casual conversation when it actually was, his big plan.

'The fourteenth? Why?' Troniya asked with an expression that, to Edy, looked like a serious frown.

'Um . . . just like that . . . nothing in particular.'

'The fourteenth . . . hmmm . . .' Troniya looked thoughtful. 'Wednesday . . . another regular day, I guess.'

'So can we meet? Same time? Same place?' Edy keenly requested.

'Um . . . maybe . . . let's see how that day goes,' Troniya said, trying to avoid eye contact.

'It's just another February day,' Edy assured her, 'I'm pretty sure things will be as fine as any other day.'

'Probably,' Troniya said, not giving him a definitive answer, which considerably vexed him.

He was forced to explain the situation to Jade later that evening for the regular analysis. After a detailed investigation on Troniya's wording and the reluctance in her expressions, the final conclusion came out to be less favourable this time.

'She's intensely tormented by something in which you undoubtedly play a major part.' Jade continued with his conclusion, 'If my interpretation of her last three sentences is right, then—' he paused, unwilling to conclude further.

'Then what?' Edy restlessly asked.

'She probably might avoid the pre-planned meeting on the fourteenth,' Jade said.

'I don't understand why she would not want to meet me when things are going just fine between us,' Edy whined.

'You did request her to meet on the fourteenth, which she knows is Valentine's Day,' Jade said. 'Hence, she must have expected you would gift her something.'

'If that's true, then she probably doesn't want you to gift her anything,' Barrie said, taking into consideration of the navy-ness that ran in her family. 'She might be thinking you are moving way too fast.'

'A reasonable explanation,' Jade said, for the first time without a counterproposal statement to Barrie's assumption, while Edy sat dumbfounded.

The fourteenth of February was no different from any of the three hundred and sixty-five days that had gone by, except that everyone knew it was yet another annually occurring, most celebrated Valentine's Day. One thing that everyone at MPS knew, including the members of the academic staff, was the secretive exchange of gifts at secretive times and secretive places.

The only reason of this secretive act was to avoid getting trapped by the stern principal or any of the fifty-odd faculty members, except of course, Miss Ashria Kaum, in which case she would only put on her usual broad smile and let the students exchange the fondly selected gifts.

The first awful news that came in as Edy entered the class on 14 February was from Mable. 'Troniya said she will not be able to meet you today,' Mable informed him.

'What? Why?' Edy asked in shock.

Mable shrugged. 'I don't know, Edy, I was only told to inform you about it.'

'Just like I told you,' Jade said, 'something's troubling her, which is why she's avoiding any meeting today.'

'Like I said,' Barrie joined in, 'she thinks you are moving too fast.'

'Now even though you ditch the gifting part, she would still avoid you, just in case, to make sure no gifts reach her,' Jade admitted.

That entire day, Edy desperately tried to secretively signal Troniya. Nothing seemed to work. All his attempts went in vain, both in class and dining hall, where they usually signalled each other with smiles. She just wouldn't look at him. Though she was well aware of Edy's hand and eye signal postures, she pretended to be totally oblivious to them.

But thanks to the commitment and the dedication that one has towards his loved one, Edy didn't quit his effort to meet her.

He waited back in the class with the two gifts that he had bought earlier that month and patiently stood at the B-door, looking through the deserted B-corridor, hoping Troniya would turn up.

What if she doesn't show up? Edy doubtfully thought at half past four.

She will! his inner voice encouraged, which for the first time, Edy felt comfortable listening to.

The B-corridor was as quiet as it could get. No footsteps could be heard as the minutes flew by.

At half past five, Edy had not moved an inch away from the B-door, peeking through the half-opened door at regular short intervals. He tightly held on to the gifts, hoping he would somehow give them to Troniya.

She will, she will, Edy thought as he took a detailed glance at the red, white, and black heart-shaped coffee cup and the tiny love book.

There's still plenty of time! his inner voice reminded him, which made Edy look at his watch.

Forty past five, he languidly sighed, still not losing his hopes.

As the clock ticked away, Edy grew restless.

If not now, he impatiently thought as he moved away from the B-door, *when else would I be able to gift her these?*

He walked to and fro across the huge hall, taking quick short steps. At a minute to six, Edy knew Troniya was not going to turn up. He had lost that thin ray of hope that he had held on to since the beginning of his two-hour long wait.

'Whatever it takes,' Edy determinedly told himself, 'I'm gonna find out the reason for her strange avoidance.'

At six, he forcefully stepped out of the A-door and sluggishly walked back to his dorm.

In a matter of a few minutes, grade 10 students were back in class for the regular two-hour evening prep. Troniya was seen studying at her own desk—row 4, desk 3.

Edy signalled her several times, but he didn't get the usual hush-hush eye response from the latter.

Did I scare her away with my suspicious request to meet on Valentine's Day? Edy thought while most of the students studiously indulged in their academic work.

Why isn't she even looking at me? he cried to himself after a dozen failed attempts to grab her attention. No matter what Edy did, Troniya remained as unresponsive as she could ever get. His deliberate tries were botched in the dining hall too as he unwillingly gulped his share of food later that evening.

'Things will be fine by morning, Edy, trust me,' Barrie consoled him after having watched his pal's innumerable unsuccessful efforts to grab Troniya's attention.

Edy weakly shook his head, with a series of regretful sighs.

'I shouldn't have done this.' He heaved another deep sigh. 'She's been made paranoid by my acts, I shouldn't have planned the gifts in the first place.'

'Cheer up, buddy,' Jade tried to encourage him. 'It's not the end of the world.'

'I already feel like I'm living in a post-apocalyptic world,' Edy obscurely uttered.

* * * * * *

The Doomed Diary

*P*icture this: One fine morning you wake up only to find out the most bizarre thing that has ever happened in your life—an upside-down world, literally.

The moment you open your eyes you understand the basic laws of physics have been twisted to such an extremity that you almost don't believe your own eyes. You realize you are facing the floor. Your cot and bed seem to be magically attached to what was previously called the roof and what you are now forced to call the floor. The running fan scares you to no end. After coping with the alarming terror visual of your surroundings, you get out of your bed.

What's even worse is when you find out the water is running up the roof. You step out of the house after spending an awful lot of time in the bathroom, not able to direct the flow of water to the precise desired point.

The world outside looks so weird that you pinch yourself to confirm you are not caught up in a strange dream. You feel the pain of the pinch as much as your eyes feel the pain of seeing the world upside-down. The roads are above your head. Buses, cars, bikes, and trains are running in the sky, upside-down. You regret leaving your house in the first place. The pukey sensation in your tummy gets much worse.

Eventually you get paranoid and run to your nearest friend's house and shout at him with all your lung power, 'What the hell happened around here?'

Your friend calmly frowns and replies, 'Nothing has happened. This is how it's always been!' The pukey sensation races from your tummy towards your chest. That is when you realize that the world is the same but the things that have happened and that are going to happen to you are what's making you feel the world is upside-down when, in fact, you are the one who's upside-down—figuratively.

Isn't this is how you would have felt when something went horribly wrong that shouldn't have gone wrong in the first place and all of a sudden you get the 'world upside-down' feeling.

Funny how the upside-down world happens only when something terrible happens.

Thursday, 15 February 2007

That very day as Edy woke up, his strong thought of *Everything is downhill from now on* was as wrong as it could have gotten. He hadn't had the slightest cue of a clue as to how uphill things were going to get, beginning from that very day.

The classes resumed at nine, but instead of the regular Miss Andrella's first hour, it was Miss Ashria Kaum who had come in. She did have her broad smile on, which did indicate that everything was as orderly as usual.

Though everyone was happy at Miss Ashria's appearance, some curious ones, including Edy, wondered why there had been a change in the timetable.

As the curiosity-driven students enquired about the irregularity of classes that morning, Miss Ashria revealed that Miss Andrella along with Miss Adeline, Miss Drusilla, and Miss Susanna were called in for a meeting by Mr Joseph.

No one, including Miss Ashria Kaum, had had a hint as to why the four teachers were called in right after the school assembly.

'Only female teachers?' Jade amusingly asked, 'Isn't that a little spooky?'

At around ten past eleven that morning, after the short coffee break, the true reason for the abnormality in the class timetable came to light.

'You won't believe what has happened back in the girls' dormitory,' Celia whined. By the look on her face, the other members of the First Benchers surely knew she was frightened.

'What happened?' Barrie concernedly asked.

'How can they ever do such things?' Mable cried as she entered the class and shut the B-door loudly.

'Can you both stop with the whining and tell us what's bothering you?' Allen requested as immense curiosity filled him.

'Not just us, all the senior girls are agitated,' Celia said.

'The senior girls' dormitory has been thoroughly searched by the four lady teachers who were called in for the meeting,' Mable revealed the awful news.

'I saw them leaving our dorm with filled bags,' Celia added.

'Why?' Barrie asked, shocked.

'We heard that Mr Joseph had ordered an inspection of the senior girls' dormitory and seized any gifts that they found,' Mable agitatedly revealed.

'Valentine's gifts,' Celia horrendously corrected.

'Are they nuts?' Allen whined, raising his brows.

'Mr Joseph definitely is to have done such a thing,' Jade added while Edy sat thanking Troniya and could have embraced her for not taking his gifts the previous day.

Could she have somehow known that this was gonna happen? Edy was submerged in deep thoughts as he quietly questioned himself, feeling grateful to Troniya. *Could it be the reason why she avoided meeting me?*

'They have confiscated every gift and every suspicious item that they could lay their hands on,' Celia heatedly said, 'like gifts, photos, letters, diaries.'

'Diaries? What diaries?' Barrie asked.

'Troniya said her personal diary was missing from her cupboard,' Mable said and Celia nodded.

'It's just a diary, what could they possibly do with a diary?' Edy said defensively.

'I don't know, but she is awfully upset with what has happened back in the dorm,' Mable said, which started to shake Edy off his confidence pillar.

'Mr Joseph's strictness is close to weirdness,' Allen commented after hearing the immoral acts of the principal.

'Our dorm has been messed up like hell,' Mable whined.

Barrie signalled Celia to make sure his gifts were not confiscated. Celia signalled back, assuring she had hidden them in a safe place.

'Isn't it just the cupboards?' Allen asked.

Mable and Celia shook their heads in dismay. 'Under beds, inside pillows, beneath blankets, unlocked baggage and suitcases and whatnot,' Mable cried.

The news of the treacherous act of Mr Joseph spread like wildfire. The rage of the students shot up to its crest.

Nobody had ever thought Mr Joseph, who was a stern character, was so very stern about the warning that he had given on the first day.

But none had the courage to enter the Chambers of Principal Authority and argue in favour of the unfortunate victims. The guilty were scared and the innocent were just not bothered. The lovebirds of MPS ended up regretting theirs acts of exchanging the V Day gifts and only hoped the punishment was not to be an indefinite suspension, not when the end-of-term exams were around the corner.

As the inspecting squad of four lady teachers returned to Mr Joseph's chamber, they uncovered the bags of items that they were able to confiscate from the senior girls' dormitory.

Miss Andrella also had a sheet that contained what item was found in whose possession. It was an instruction of Mr Joseph that was only carried out by Miss Andrella.

The four teachers emptied the plastic bags to reveal different kinds of V Day gifts along with letters that were of different sizes and colours, photos of random guys. There were countless greeting cards, most of which had a 'from' and 'to' written on them, which made it all the more easy to pin down the exact dispatcher and the recipient.

After all the confiscated items were piled up in the cupboard, Miss Andrella had one last item left in her bag. Just like everyone saves the best piece for last, she too had saved the most interesting item that she had found in the dormitory.

It was the black-leather-finished diary that belonged to Troniya. Miss Andrella carefully placed the diary on Mr Joseph's glass-topped table as the other three teachers stared at it with curiosity.

On seeing it, Mr Joseph wondered which of the boys of MPS was so studious to gift a book as a V Day gift.

'Is this a Valentine's gift too?' Mr Joseph asked as he took a closer look at the golden carvings on the smooth surface of the diary.

'No, sir, it's a personal diary that I found in one of the girls' cupboards,' Miss Andrella eagerly said.

'Why have you confiscated a personal diary?' Mr Joseph asked as he read through the golden words 'PERSONAL DIARY – 2006' carved on it.

'The content of the diary is what has forced me to confiscate it, sir. I sincerely request you to read all of it to get a clearer picture of what has been happening in our school,' Miss Andrella said.

The other three teachers in the chamber were now craving to read what was written in it; so was Mr Joseph. The words 'personal diary' are so mysteriously eye-catching that even the laziest person on this planet would want to read it, without missing one single word.

Mr Joseph, who was baffled on hearing Miss Andrella, was forced to open the diary. As he did, he came across the deadly curse that Ray Anderson and Eric Reez had come across when they were doing their unethical acts back in grade 10.

He read through the written curse and felt even more spellbound. But as he continued, he felt the intense urge of the staring teachers to lay their hands upon the diary. He wanted to read the diary alone, peacefully, and wanted to get rid of the curious staring eyes.

'You all have done a very good job. I sincerely appreciate your cooperation. Thank you!' Mr Joseph full-heartedly thanked the teachers.

'Thank you, sir,' the teachers replied and forcefully left the chamber.

Fortunately for Miss Andrella, she had read the entire contents of the diary even without missing the part that explained Miss Andrella's anger on the students or Mr Joseph's infamous sternness among various other known and unknown facts.

By the time Mr Joseph had read the last page, Miss Andrella had already leaked its contents to the three other curious inspecting squad members, who in turn leaked it to the other faculty members. Now that Miss Andrella's 'tickling in tummy' feeling had sunk down, she kept her mouth shut while the unfortunate news spread from mouth to mouth. It didn't take more than a couple of short hours for the news to fall into Edy's ears.

'What are you talking about?' Edy tetchily asked.

'That's what I heard back in the academic staff chambers while I was passing by,' Mable revealed.

'What's so obnoxious about a personal diary? What contents are you talking about?' Edy asked.

'The most surprising of all, your name in it.' Mable recollected the words that she had heard from the academic staff chambers.

'*My name?*' Edy freaked out as his heart pounded at a hundred and forty.

Mable nodded while Jade and Barrie sat speechless.

'You're kidding, right?' Allen asked as he was the only other person who was as shocked to hear the news as Edy. He was under the assumption that they all were still trying to lure him into the practical joke.

'Allen, this is serious,' Celia said with a bright frown.

'Seriously? The diary contains my name?' Edy asked again, still not believing what he had heard.

'At least that's what I heard,' Mable said.

Right then, Edy knew whom he had to approach to gather more information on the matter. He hurriedly rushed to Miss Ashria Kaum's cubicle. On reaching the door, she welcomed him as though she had been expecting him for quite some time. Her diluted smile was the first sign that things were not going quite well.

'I'm sure you already know the bad news,' Miss Ashria Kaum said as Edy shut the door behind him.

'Ma'am,' Edy said with a worried look. 'All that know is that diary contains my name.' He fearfully asked, 'Is there anything more that you can tell me, please?'

'Well,' Miss Ashria started, lowering her voice as she revealed the bits and pieces that she knew, 'I did hear from one of the inspecting teachers that the diary contained a lot of information.'

'Information on?' Edy restlessly interrupted.

'All the meetings you have had with her till date'

'*What?*' Edy moaned as sheer panic set in him.

Miss Ashria Kaum said, for the first time without her legendary smile, 'I know it's a shocking bit, but it's true, all the meetings you both have ever had, sentence by sentence and word by word, in every possible detail.'

Edy dumped his burning forehead into his cup-shaped palms. 'Has Mr Joseph read it?' Edy worriedly asked.

'Well . . . the confiscated diary is in his possession now, so yes, that's likely.'

'I'm so dead,' Edy faintly sighed.

'That diary does contain enough proof to trigger a suspension order and possibly restrain you both from appearing from the end-of-term examination.'

Edy looked up at Miss Ashria Kaum; his eyes showcased a good deal of fear.

'But, ma'am, we were just friends,' he said in defence. 'I will convey that to Mr Joseph before all of this goes out of hand.'

'You could, but why would there be so much of detailed writing about the meetings if you both were just friends?' Miss Ashria Kaum reminded him. 'That's the question you want to answer before defending yourselves.'

Edy put his head down again and worriedly thought, *What have I done?*

'Ma'am, is there anything at all you can do to help her?' Edy asked, more concerned about Troniya.

'Had it been our previous principal, I would have been able to, but Mr Joseph—' Miss Ashria sternly shook her head.

'I wish I could at least save Troniya from all the embarrassment that she is going to face,' Miss Ashria continued, showing much concern for the lead victim. 'You do know how well news of this kind spreads in MPS, I wouldn't be shocked if a grade 2 student comes up to me and asks about the diary.'

'What if she's suspended?' Edy cried to himself.

'Let's pray and hope for the best,' Miss Ashria said. 'At least let's not hope for the worst.'

Edy's heart sank to his feet. His quick-witted brain was now jammed with all possible punishments that Troniya might have to face. He accused himself for having lured Troniya into such humiliation.

'If only someone could convince Mr Joseph,' Miss Ashria Kaum sighed in dismay.

Edy hastily went back to his class and joined his tiny group, who were waiting for the news. The only person who was more shocked on hearing Edy was Allen.

I still don't believe these guys, Allen thought as he quietly listened to what looked like a serious school-life drama. *But I'm starting to wonder why s are they trying so hard just to make me believe there's a secret affair going on between Edy and Troniya,* Allen thought again at the end of the horrid story.

Edy looked back at row 4, desk 3. Troniya's absence in the class troubled him like a child being troubled by nightmares.

'Where's Troniya?' he anxiously asked.

'She's back in the dorm,' Celia confirmed.

*   *   *   *   *   *

Back in the senior girls' dormitory, Troniya was drenched in disbelief. She knew there were innumerous misfortunes galloping towards her as she could already feel the harshness of the incoming inescapable troubles.

If enduring Mr Joseph's remorseless punishment was one part, facing her dad was the other part—the major part. Going through an intense load of humiliation was entirely another part that she knew she would have to face.

As she sat with her face hidden in her cupped hands, she could only think of one possible solution, which was, anyway, not very foolproof. A plea request to Mr Hal was what she could now think of. Mr Hal, who had a soft spot for Troniya, like a bunch of other faculty members, admired her not only for her exceptionally good academic performance but also for her diligent work in the Academic Club.

Without wasting another minute, Troniya approached Mr Hal, who was in his own cubicle in the staff chambers. He had already been feeling sorry for what had happened. She pleaded him to help her from the possible suspension. As Mr Hal's beloved student beseeched him with utmost sincerity, he couldn't deny her frantic request and finally agreed to talk to Mr Joseph about it.

Without knowing how on earth he would ever be able to convince the stern principal, Mr Hal entered the Chambers of Principal Authority. He only entered the principal's chamber to discuss matters that concerned either him or his work and mostly when he wanted Mr Joseph to take disciplinary actions against students' indiscipline, like he had done regarding Edy only a few weeks ago.

But as he entered Mr Joseph's chamber, he realized he had, for the first time ever, stepped forward to speak in favour of a student—first time ever to attempt such a feat by Mr Hal. Mr Joseph welcomed Mr Hal with a smile. Though it was a rare sight, he did smile when in company with his closest associates.

'What brings you to my office, Mr Hal?' Mr Joseph asked, still smiling as he paused his paperwork.

'Um . . . I . . . I'm here . . .' Mr Hal hesitantly mumbled, adjusting his decade-old spectacles, 'I'm here to talk about the diary, sir.'

Mr Joseph's smiling face instantly turned aggravated. 'What more is remaining to speak on it?' Mr Joseph continued coarsely, 'I don't want anyone to comment on it or speak in favour of anyone. I would only like to deal with those who are solely involved in this case.'

Mr Joseph paused as he dumped a stack of paper into the opened drawer that contained the ill-fated diary. 'The guilty will be severely dealt with,' he added.

'But, sir, Troniya is irreproachable. She is such a studious and scholarly student that not a single teacher has ever found fault with her,' Mr Hal admitted as honestly as he could. 'Just because she was lured into this nuisance, it's not fair to deal with this so harshly.'

'So you think the whole blunder is only Edy's and she has absolutely no role in this?' Mr Joseph calmly questioned.

A deep silence fell upon both the debaters. That specific statement had left Mr Hal wordless. Mr Joseph had put forward a question that was practically inarguable.

'Here,' Mr Joseph said as he revealed the diary from the table locker. 'You read it and tell me if I should spare those two.'

Mr Hal opened the diary and swiftly read through the parts that narrated every meeting that had taken place, every word in the conversation accompanied by the detailed emotional expressions and responses.

As Mr Hal read through the last page, which narrated the story where Edy had requested Troniya to meet him on the fourteenth of February, he let out a deep, regretful sigh.

'For every action, there is an equal and opposite reaction,' Mr Joseph continued, taking the diary back into his possession. 'Without Troniya's involvement, this matter wouldn't have got this far today. She could have, by all means, avoided it.'

He put the diary back into the table locker, where it helplessly lay in the darkness.

'She has been and she is involved in this very case and that attracts a huge penalty,' he pointed out, "And all this has happened despite my warning on the very first day"

Mr Hal sat numb. Of course it didn't demand a PhD in criminology for one to decode the contents of the diary; neither did it require a high degree of interpretation skills.

'I'm not supporting Edy, at the same time I'm not accusing only Troniya,' Mr Joseph said. 'Both have played equal roles in committing this mistake, so both will be accused and punished accordingly.' Mr Joseph's arguments and statements only sounded more and more acceptable as Mr Hal sat listening to the former.

'One mistake shouldn't form the basis to judge a person who's always been so decorous, sir,' Mr Hal put forward his views in a lowered voice. 'And she has always been disciplined and has abided by the rules and regulations of this institution, among various other scholarly traits.'

'I'm sorry, Mr Hal,' Mr Joseph said, 'I cannot deal this on a case-by-case basis, which would only mean I'm being biased to few students.'

As Mr Hal heard the stubborn principal's final decision, he, without arguing any further, left the chamber, disappointedly.

Troniya heard from the computer teacher about his unsuccessful attempt to save her from the dire punishment. Her only hope had hit a dead end. She knew she had to face all the severe consequences. Her fear dominated all other emotions as she thought about facing her dad, should the principal order an indefinite suspension. Her mind was in total chaos. She knew she had jeopardized both her academic career as well as her outstanding reputation, because of her past acts.

* * * * * *

The Spiteful Truths

'*I*van's involved in this,' Mable said, starting to reveal what she had learned from Troniya.

'Ivan?' Jade and Edy asked spontaneously.

'Why am I not surprised?' Barrie asked, on hearing about Ivan's shocking involvement. Allen, who now believed all that he had thought was a practical joke was not, in fact, a practical joke, sat still, listening to the others.

Mable nodded and revealed further in detail all about Ivan's diabolic involvement that she had learned from Troniya.

Friday, 19 January 2007

'So how are things going on with you?' Ivan asked Troniya as the classroom emptied for the short coffee break.

'As usual,' Troniya replied in a cursory manner as she walked towards the B-door, accompanied by Irennica.

'I mean the newer things.'

'What newer things?' Troniya asked and stopped herself from exiting the B-door.

'I bet you know what I'm talking about,' Ivan said.

'No, I don't,' Troniya said irritably and stepped out, ignoring Ivan's silly talk, like always.

'The secret meetings?' Ivan's words brought Troniya's exiting plan to an abrupt halt. She waved at Irennica to go ahead and walked back towards Ivan.

'What are you talking about?' Troniya asked with a serious frown.

'The secret meetings that you and our class representative are having in the evenings,' Ivan said and put on his smug smile like he had stumbled upon a heap of top-secret bundles.

'I think you got the wrong info,' Troniya defended herself.

Ivan confidentially shook his head, still having the smug look on his face. 'We both know what's happening in this class and you know that that I know about it.'

'How do you know?' Troniya asked as restlessness set in. She only tried to hide her agitated emotions by putting on a 'not a big deal' expression.

'I can't tell you that,' Ivan said, which angered Troniya to no end, 'but I'm pretty sure I know every detail of every meeting that's been happening between you both.'

'That's impossible,' Troniya defended herself, showing her fake smile.

'Honey, you can try and defend all you want.' Ivan sounded more confident than ever. 'But I know all about your newfound secret crush that you have had recently.'

Troniya was left speechless. After a quick thoughtful second, she realized the reason behind his confidence.

He's been reading my diary, Troniya thought, and it boiled her blood. She flared up her nose at his immoral acts. *What a jerk!* she thought again as she stared at him with immense anger.

'But you don't have to worry. Your little secret is safe with me,' Ivan said.

'Whatever!' Troniya frantically said and quickly exited the classroom.

*   *   *   *   *   *

'So Ivan had been reading Troniya's diary,' Jade started to speak up after Mable had finished with a part of what she had in mind. 'That's how he knows every detail of all the meetings you have had.'

'Which is why she decided to shift the diary from class to the dormitory,' Mable added.

Edy's rage-filled eyes stared at the wall ahead as he listened to the foul acts of Ivan. He clenched his teeth hard and tightened his fist as the scene of Ivan troubling Troniya flashed through his disturbed mind.

'That's not all,' Mable said before starting to reveal the second part of her findings as everyone keenly turned to listen to her.

Thursday, 8 February 2007

'It's none of my business but I was just wondering if Edy has asked you to meet on the fourteenth?' Ivan asked Troniya, who was already pissed off with Ivan's immoral acts of stalking her personal life. The diary that was the gateway to all her personal details was now hidden in her cupboard, safe and sound from any intruders.

'It's none of your business, Ivan,' Troniya calmly said. 'Stop bothering me'.

'I'm just trying to be friends with you, okay?' Ivan said with a sorry look on his devilish face.

'No, he hasn't, why?' Troniya said, avoiding looking at him. She knew it was of no use to hide anything from him, from someone who already knew every bit of the details.

'Well, it's the fourteenth,' Ivan said, sounding as though he was really concerned about her well-being, 'Valentine's Day, so I was guessing he might have asked you to meet . . . um . . . you know . . . to gift you the V Day gifts.

'So?' Troniya petulantly questioned, 'What's the big deal in that? It's totally his wish.'

'It's not the gifts that I'm worried about,' Ivan started to unleash his pre-planned sly trick on her, 'but the size of the gifts that came in was a shocker.'

'Size?' Troniya, who had been carefully listening to his last sentence, asked.

'They are enormous,' Ivan lied, putting on his best fake concerned look. 'He has bought you a huge greeting card, about this size.' He spread out his arms to form a width of about two and half feet. 'And two huge heart-shaped photo frames and a giant collage, I suppose,' Ivan lied, putting in as many minute details as he could to make it sound realistic. 'I didn't get a clear view of it though.'

'How do you know?' Troniya suspiciously questioned.

'I'm his neighbour in our dorm and I saw him hiding it in his recently emptied black suitcase above his cupboard.' Ivan said, pinpointing the small details of his imaginary scene that helped in luring Troniya into believing Ivan's imaginary gifts.

'And he's gonna give every one of those to you on the fourteenth,' Ivan started explaining his fake concerns, 'which means you would have to carry them back to your dormitory, which would in turn catch the inescapable attention and curiosity of the passers-by.' He paused as Troniya pictured the scene in her thought-filled mind.

'It could be your friends or unfortunately any of the fifty faculty members or, more regrettably, Mr Joseph, who always happens to inspect anything noticeably suspicious around him.' He continued to implement his devilish plan as Troniya stared at the wall ahead. 'Then you will have to reveal your little secret to them, which would naturally lead to the wrecking of Edy's respectful image that he has tiresomely earned over the years.'

Having pictured the chaotic scene that Ivan had explained, Troniya realized how troublesome it would get for Edy, should Mr Joseph or any one of the teachers, excluding, of course, Miss Ashria Kaum, get to know about the V Day gifts.

'Like I said, it's none of my business,' Ivan disturbed a thought-filled Troniya, 'but I was only concerned about you and I hate to see you facing preventable trouble, having known I could have stopped you from it.'

Troniya didn't move an inch, still staring at the wall ahead.

'You are a good friend of mine and so is Edy,' he said again, with a much sweeter voice. 'I just want to help you both from falling into grave danger.'

Troniya shifted her gaze at him after hearing what Ivan had said about saving Edy from grave danger.

'What do you suggest I do?' Troniya, who was more worried about Edy, asked.

'Well,' Ivan said, still faking his immense concernedness. 'The only way out is to avoid meeting him on the fourteenth,' he continued with a deep, convincing voice. 'In that way we can be sure he will not be able to give you those gifts at all.'

Troniya went back to deep thinking as Ivan suggested his version of a safety plan.

'By which you would have not only saved yourself but Edy as well.' He paused.

'Is that all?' asked Troniya, who now seemed more comfortable talking to him.

'Yup, that would be all . . . and, um,' Ivan quickly said, 'he might try, by all means possible, to meet you on the fourteenth, you might have to deny all his requests and avoid his signals and pleadings.' He paused and looked at her. 'I know it's hard to deliberately ignore someone but . . . you have to do it just for a day.' At this point, he knew his diabolic plan had worked more easily than he had expected.

'That's the only way you have in order to save him from losing his hard-earned badge of office,' he said and waited for a reply.

Troniya gently nodded, agreeing to his plan. 'I'm still wondering why you are helping me with this,' she said.

'Troniya, we have always been good friends, haven't we?' he said with a deep, fake, friendly smile. 'Even though sometimes we have had to go through rough patches for which I take full responsibility.'

'Well, thank you for that!' Troniya said and smiled, which she hadn't done for quite a long time when Ivan was around.

'And by the way,' Ivan stopped Troniya for a second time, 'when he asks why you had not met with him, you might want to use a cover story in order to bury any suspicion . . . and I would suggest you keep my name out of it.'

'Why?'

'Ah . . . how do I put this?' He looked thoughtful for a second and then said, 'I really don't want him to know I have been involved in changing your thoughts, considering he feels I'm nothing short of an enemy.'

'That's not true. He doesn't have any enemies,' Troniya defended Edy.

'Oh . . . you don't know much about the previous year fights, do you?'

'Fights?'

'Only so many . . . the best was Bryan's.'

* * * * * *

'And you were wondering who had revealed Bryan's story to her,' Barrie said. Edy looked furious; his teeth clenched harder and fist tightened further.

'And that is why she was so reluctant when you asked her to meet on the fourteenth?' Jade said, feeling sorry for his enraged neighbour. 'And she deliberately avoided all your signals in the class as well as in the dining hall.'

'So, basically, he's the reason for all the awful things that have been happening to you,' Allen spoke out for the first time since the start of Mable's narration. Edy's breaths became shorter and shallower as he was angered by Ivan's sinful acts.

'He's so bloody jealous,' Barrie sighed.

'That's not all,' Mable said—that grabbed back everyone's attention except Edy's as he furiously gazed at the wall ahead.

'Troniya also said Eric and Ray might be involved too,' Mable said.

'Eric and Ray?' Allen, Jade, and Barrie asked simultaneously.

'She said they both have been giving her weird looks right after she shifted her diary to the dorm,' Mable said.

'Can someone go get Ray and Eric?' Edy said in a deep, husky, frightening voice.

'I'm on it,' Allen said and jumped up from his desk. 'What about Ivan?'

'Just the two,' Edy insisted.

'This has all gone so wrong,' Jade said after Allen rushed out to find the intruders.

Barrie put his arm around Edy's shoulders, 'You all right?'

Edy sighed and put his hands over his head, grabbing onto his hair with frustration.

Soon, Allen returned with Eric and Ray. They both looked awful, with fear driving their thoughts. Ray took a gulp as he saw the furiousness in Edy's burning eyes.

'Tell us everything you know,' Barrie, who now looked equally agitated, demanded.

In sheer fear, Eric and Ray honestly revealed their immoral acts, beginning from how they had encountered the personal diary till the day right when it mysteriously disappeared.

'And all of a sudden, the diary wasn't there anymore,' Eric said at the end of his narration.

'We searched her desk thoroughly but couldn't find it,' Ray, the partner in crime, supported his pal's statement. 'So we forgot about it, until yesterday when we heard it was confiscated by Mr Joseph.'

Eric's and Ray's revelation turned out to be the most surprising of all revelations that anyone in the tiny group had ever come across. The details were so accurately precise that even Edy couldn't believe his own ears. By now Edy knew how important he had become to Troniya. The news about his name in the personal diary alone was sufficient for him to have known how indispensable he had become to his lady love.

'She loves me!' Edy faintly murmured to himself while Allen had surprisingly wide-open eyes. 'Troniya loves me, she loves me, Troniya loves—'

'Was Ivan involved too?' Barrie strictly questioned Eric and Ray after having digested his share of the surprise that came in from their big revelation.

Eric and Ray looked at each other and shook their heads. 'We don't know anything about Ivan being involved in this,' Eric said.

'Probably he was reading it at a different time,' Jade suggested.

'If only Ivan had not been so jealous of you both,' Mable said to a furious Edy. His temper had shot up to his head. He stood up with a lot of force even as the others wondered what to do next.

'Where's Ivan?' he asked, which brought a swift reply from Allen.

'I saw him back in the dorm when I had gone to fetch Eric and Ray.'

'Edy?' Barrie called out as Edy got up from his desk.

'What's he up to?' Allen asked, and nobody answered.

'Edy, wait,' Barrie pleaded. Nothing seemed to have passed his ears as he wrathfully made his way out of the A-door.

A worried Allen, Jade, and Barrie quickly followed behind to stop whatever Edy planned on doing to Ivan.

'Edy? Where are you going?' Allen shouted on seeing Edy at the corridor's exit.

'He's not listening,' Jade pointed out and they quickly jogged on the route that led them to the senior boys' dormitory.

Like a bullet shot out of a shotgun, Edy entered the dorm and even before the following three could make it to the entrance, he reappeared out of the door, like a heated bull, dragging Ivan out by his collar.

'This is not good,' Jade said as the three were now galloping on the route that led to the boys' restroom. From a distance, they could see Edy mercilessly dragging his new-made enemy without bothering to listen to Ivan's begging.

'Wait, please, listen to me,' Ivan beseeched even as he tripped several times on the cemented floor. 'I can explain everything, wait, where are you taking me?'

All those who had seen Edy grabbing Ivan by the collar back in the dorm, including seniors from grade 11 and grade 12, knew it was going to be yet another famous bathroom brawl. They followed the lead, almost right behind.

'Look there—Edy and Ivan,' Rodney shouted and all those on the grounds witnessed the infrequent sight of someone being ruthlessly dragged to the bathroom.

'Let's roll,' Jeoff suggested and another large pro-violence group quickly followed.

In the bathroom, clusters of a hooting mob gathered around a fuming Edy and a frightened Ivan Anderson, who was still trying to convince Edy to listen. But the noise of loud howling and yelling made his desperate cry for mercy almost inaudible.

Edy forcefully pushed his victim onto one of the surrounding walls, simultaneously having released the latter's collar. On Ivan's collision with the wall, there was a loud thudding noise that sparked off an even louder roar from the forty-odd surrounding students.

'Yeah, that's what I'm talking about,' a violence fan shouted out with his eyes wide open and hands raised in encouragement. Even before Ivan could completely recover from the impact of the collision, Edy unleashed his fury as his hard, tightened fists' blows fell upon Ivan's face.

'*Yeah, yeah, more punches, punch him on the nose!*' another pro-violence spectator, who also happened to be one of many Ivan haters, yelped at the top of his voice.

'Please listen to me,' Ivan cried his lungs out, but all his pleading went in vain. His wail for help was far too outnumbered by forty-odd hooting voices.

More punches followed and Ivan only begged louder, 'For God's sake, stop punching and listen to me.' All he could do was to try and block the unpitying incoming blows from his maddened partner. Though he was successful in avoiding a few on his face, most of them ended up right on his nose.

Thud, thud, thud, more punches' noise emanated as the attack continued.

As Edy withdrew his tightened fist after several punches on Ivan's red and shapeless nose; blood soon gushed out from both his broken nose and cut lips. The white T-shirt that Ivan had worn was now painted in red. The colour ran from his neck down all the way to his waist. Tears poured out straight away.

'Look at him cry like a baby.' Rodney pointed his finger and the mob laughed out.

Edy grabbed hold of Ivan's blood-drenched collar and drew him closer as the hooligan-like behaviour from the mob continued.

'Now you listen to me,' Edy said with a terrorizing look on his face that frightened even Barrie. The shouting receded, which made the loud voice more audible to the audience.

'Now you listen to me carefully,' Edy repeated with a more repulsive voice and said, *'I love Troniya and Troniya loves me.'* His voice sounded like thunderclaps and the words reverberated though the lengthy bathroom corridor and the cheering mob calmed down further.

'No one can and no one will ever take that away from us' he shouted loudly. Ivan's eyes were only half opened and he largely depended on Edy's arm strength to stand straight. 'Do you get it?' Edy bellowed, and the faint shock waves of the sound dribbled onto Ivan's bleeding face.

After having heard the thunderclap-like words, Ivan faintly nodded. The cheering mob hooted and howled at Ivan's surrender agreement. Edy soon let go of the blood-drenched collar and Ivan dropped down like a lifeless branch falling off a tree, bringing another thudding noise.

'One more time,' Edy said, angrily pointing his finger at his victim, 'one more time you try and talk to Troniya—' Before he could complete his threatening warning, Ivan chose to speak. 'I won't . . . I swear . . . I won't,' he cried, hiding his bloody face in his palm.

Barrie had never before seen Edy that furious. It surely meant one thing—that he was utterly and sincerely serious about Troniya.

'Now, where are Eric and Ray?' Edy called out in a voice that again terrorized Ivan.

'Second round,' Jeoff and Rodney yelled, and the mob was back to life with more whooping. 'Somebody drag in Eric and Ray,' Jeoff suggested.

Edy hastily made his way after having decided to drag them in on his own. The pro-violence mob followed, leaving behind a badly beaten-up Ivan alone on the wet bathroom floor.

'Edy, that's enough, stop it already,' Barrie pleaded as he ran behind to stop his friend, after having made his way through the restless mob.

'Is this the guy I was messing around with all these days?' Allen asked in a low, scared voice. 'I didn't know about his terrifying short-temperedness.'

'Well, you do know now,' Jade said, hurriedly pacing towards the senior boys' dorm, 'so you better think twice before picking on him.'

'If that doesn't help, then just imagine you being in Ivan's place,' Rodney, who had heard them, suggested with a brief laugh.

Edy forcefully entered the dorm after having freed himself from the clutches of Barrie's weak hands. The news of the bathroom scene had already spread to the senior boys' dorm, where Eric and Ray hid in fear.

A frightened Ray stood behind Eric as Edy approached them. Barrie followed closely, still trying to pacify his best pal. In a blink of an eye, Eric's collar was held on to, with the strength of an industrial metal clipper.

'Edy, stop,' Barrie commanded. 'Your arrogance has no meaning, and it was only Ivan's fault and not Eric and Ray's.'

'There's no reason for me to spare these two. They have made a mistake,' Edy angrily said and started to pull Eric towards the entrance door.

'There is,' Barrie said again, loudening his voice. 'Isn't it because of these two that you learnt all that was in the diary?' Barrie questioned, standing in Edy's way. 'Isn't it because of these two that you learnt about Troniya's love for you?'

Edy abruptly stopped a step away from the dormitory exit door.

'We do agree what we did was not morally right,' Eric admitted in a pleading manner, 'but we didn't mean to cause any harm to her.'

'And we are not the reason for all your troubles,' Ray joined in, still taking cover behind Eric. 'Please spare us, considering it's because of us that you learnt about all her secret thoughts on you.'

Edy instantly released the tightly gripped collar. Taking a deep breath, he exhaled all his temper out and closed his eyes as he took control over his anger.

*   *   *   *   *   *

That evening, Mr Hal was called by Mr Joseph Matthew. After much arguing with himself, Mr Hal finally decided to meet the principal and uninterestedly made his way to the Chambers of Principal Authority.

'You must be wondering why I have called you,' Mr Joseph said soon after the computer teacher had entered the principal's chamber.

Mr Hal's previous encounter with the stern principal had turned out to be a rather rough one, which was the reason for his reluctance to speak up.

'This is regarding the confiscated diary,' the stern principal said, and signalled the aged teacher to take his seat. 'I have had several requests that came in today from different faculty members and department heads regarding the diary case.' Mr Joseph paused and removed his spectacles before placing them on the green-coloured glass table top.

'They all wanted me to look into it again, before making any further move on it.'

Mr Hal's eyes widened as he keenly listened to the principal.

'Most surprising of the requests came in from Portions Planning Committee head Mr Hone and from the head of Examination Conducting Committee, Mr Garth, the other teachers being Miss Ashria Kaum and Mr Sam Fisher.'

Mr Hal smiled within, as a bright ray of hope glittered in him.

'With so many requests coming in, I realized I had to have a second opinion on it as it's not very coincidental to have so many faculty members and department heads supporting a single student.' He paused momentarily.

'There has to be some serious positive testimony on Troniya.' He paused again, and after about three seconds of hesitating, he said, 'So I have decided not to proceed any further with this case.'

Mr Hal's inner smile showed up on his wrinkly face.

'I will stop it right here and let those two be guilty of their mistakes,' Mr Joseph said, even though he didn't seem very happy about what he had said.

'Truth and honesty always triumph, sir,' Mr Hal said with a lot of contentment. 'Your decision of pardon will certainly have a more positive outcome than a severe punishment would have had,' he said and happily left the chambers, heading out to inform Troniya about the good news.

Troniya, who had abandoned all hopes and was trying to find a plausible explanation to her dad, looked awkwardly miserable from all the exhaustion. She was drenched in gratification when she heard from Mr Hal about the principal's decision to pardon her.

She, who was in grave pre-depression state as worry had gnawed upon her happiness, was now out of her fear. In her excitement, she promised Mr Hal that she would never again let anyone influence her thinking and that she would only focus on building her career.

The very next day, as per Mr Joseph's academic plan, all the grade 10 and grade 12 students were sent back home for two weeks. Mr Joseph who always did things differently, spared few days for the students for end of term's preparations.

*　*　*　*　*　*

An Untimely End

Sunday, 4 March 2007

*K*nock, knock, knock.

'Are you awake, honey?' Edy's mom called out from behind the locked bedroom door.

Edy, who was still leaning on his study table, jerked and opened his eyes at a snail's pace. He had almost forgotten what he had held in his hand, when he, for the second time that morning, read the wording that was visible on the coffee cup that he had held on to all night long.

'Yes, Mom!' he replied in a deep, husky voice.

'Breakfast is ready, come down quickly, we're getting late.' His mom's voice floated through the door and her footsteps faded away into the hallway.

The scorching rays of the sun had warmed up his dull face. He gently got up, stepping on the completely dried tear pool and looked into the mirror. He realized how miserable he looked from not stepping out of his room for two full weeks.

After a sluggish shower and deliberately skipping his breakfast, he feebly loaded the small luggage onto their car and soon they were doing 80 mph on Highway 377/B.

'Edy, we do know how important the coming exams are for your academic career, but don't strain yourself to this extent. Look at you,' his mom whined. 'You look wretched from staying up all night for two weeks.'

'We know your past performance, Edy,' his dad joined in. 'Don't stress out yourself, work within your capacity. We have always been proud of you.'

'And we will always be,' his mom said with much concern for her son's weak appearance. 'You do remember the discussion we had back at home last week, don't you?'

Edy shallowly smiled and nodded, feeling guilty for not revealing to them the true reason behind his plight.

I have got only three weeks left to set things right for Troniya, he thought but wasn't sure how he would do it as only a handful of tomorrows remained.

Back in MPS, things were heated up with the start of end-of-term exams as the students got busier with their books, except of course Edy. His seriousness on the ongoing end-of-term exams only diminished over time while abundant inclusive thoughts kept him busy all day and all night.

All that he now wished for was to try and talk to Troniya and apologize for all that had happened, which he well knew was not going to help her in any way.

For three days straight, he desperately tried to signal to her over and over. All his attempts to get her attention were in vain. It was like a con trying to get justice's attention. She wouldn't even look at him.

But that didn't suppress his faith in his abilities as he took it to the next level. His frail attempts were seen in dining hall too, and when his signals became all the more conspicuous, Troniya finally gave in and took one quick, very spontaneous glance at him before going back to ignoring him all over again.

'She looked at me,' Edy whispered, not minding his surroundings. 'She did,' he said and tried to peer through the blocking heads.

'Edy, stop, the dining supervisors are right next to us,' Barrie pointed out. 'You don't want to get their attention now.'

Edy peered and more signals came up as though he hadn't heard Barrie's warning about the inspecting supervisors.

'She saw me. I'll try and signal her once more.' Edy said, not paying attention to the dining supervisors passing by. Nothing happened for the next thirty minutes, except the desperate signals that Edy was giving out.

It wasn't until the next evening that Edy realized how hard Troniya was trying to avoid him, when she was missing from her usual place in the dining area.

'Where did she go?' Edy cried as he swung his eyes from corner to corner, thoroughly searching the far-end tables. 'Has she skipped dinner?' he asked himself, after which he felt the flimsy nudge from his pal.

'Look, there she is,' Barrie said, pointing his eyes at a farther located table, where Troniya was seated with her back towards them. 'She's clearly trying to avoid seeing you and your signals,' Barrie pointed out.

'No, that can't be true!' Edy disbelievingly defended himself as the queasiness in his stomach got worse. 'Maybe the supervisors changed the seating for a day or two.'

Barrie didn't speak further, knowing his words would only upset his friend all the more. As the days passed by,

Edy quickly realized how wrong he was and how right Barrie was, when on the third consecutive day, Troniya hadn't shifted back to her previous place aka 'sweet spot'.

Even that hadn't completely shattered Edy's dying hopes. He decided he would try and talk to her in class on the next alternate no-exam day. Five minutes before Edy's pre-planned move to make his approach in front of the whole class, Miss Ashria Kaum came in with shocking news.

She secretively revealed that Mr Joseph had assigned two spies in the class, who were to keep track of any conversation between them.

'Should there be any meeting between you both, the unknown spies will escalate the issue to the principal,' Miss Ashria Kaum worriedly warned, 'after which the issue would get out of hand all over again.

'I don't care,' Edy said to his small group of five right after Miss Ashria Kaum had left.

'Edy, no,' Barrie insisted, blocking him by standing in his way.

'Out of my way, Barrie,' Edy commanded and pushed his best friend as the others watched in disbelief.

'Edy,' Mable called out. Her voice had turned scarier and more commanding than Edy's. 'Don't you know it's because of her that you are saved from possible suspension?' Mable said, angered by the irrational move that Edy had made on Barrie and that he was going to make on Troniya.

'Knowing it was because of Troniya that you are able to appear for the end-of-term exams, is this how you want to repay her?' Mable asked, which stopped Edy from getting up from his desk. 'You want to put her back in her trouble basket, go ahead, go and talk to her while the spies escalate the matter to Mr Joseph.'

Edy dropped onto his bench with closed eyes. Mable's words were now helping him to think straight, an act that he wasn't able to perform soon after the diary was confiscated. Barrie signalled Mable a thank you with his eyes.

'Not just that,' Jade joined to put forward his predictions. 'Your move would affect her performance in the exams as well,' Jade said, reminding him about Troniya's midterm performance. 'You do remember what happened on the last exam of the midterm, don't you?'

'She's had a hard time pulling herself back in and being what she had always been,' Mable worriedly cried. 'Any false move you make is a definite trouble trap for her more than you.'

'Then I'll never get to talk to her again,' Edy cried in a faint voice. 'I'll never be able to apologize to her.'

'We can try and think of a way for that,' Jade suggested.

'I'll try and convince her to talk to you when no one's around,' Mable assured him, and Celia joined in, 'Having a little patience is the key to everything, Edy.'

'I'm sorry, Barrie,' Edy apologized with a sincere sorry look.

'I thought we promised we'd never use that word between us,' Barrie smiled, patting his pal.

'Now revision,' Jade reminded, 'we have a rather tricky one tomorrow.'

Another stressful week passed. No favourable news came in from Mable as no amount of convincing had triggered a change of opinion in Troniya.

I'm losing her. Edy was maddened on this thought as cavernous anxiety gnawed on his peace of mind. He felt as though his life was ebbing away from his clutches.

Friday, 16 March 2007

It was another alternate no-exam day on the sixteenth of March and things didn't seem quite right back in grade

10. As Edy searched row 4, desk 3, he only found Irennica sitting. The absence of Troniya had made him anxious. An hour later, there was still no sign of her. Angst had shot up his brain as he constantly worried about her absence.

After a desperate enquiry with Mable, he learnt that she too was only as ignorant on her strange absence as was he.

'Is she in some kind of trouble again?' he asked Mable, who then promised to check on her. Even before Mable could step out of the class, Celia came in with the reason for Troniya's absence. Edy's distressed expression became more vivid as he heard from Celia.

'What do you mean she's sick?' he cried. 'She was well yesterday.'

'Well, I checked on her a few minutes ago. She said she was down with fever.' Celia dolefully said and panic quickly set in on Edy. His extreme concern for her forced him to help her in any way possible.

If only I could do something, anything to help her! he dejectedly thought.

The certainty of him not being able to help her out, crumbled his sanguinity further and he became inconsolably upset about Troniya's ill health. Just as everyone knows who to turn to when all paths of hopes are barricaded, Edy too knew he had only one thing he could do at this miserable point of time.

He hurriedly paced through the now thick and bloomed garden path, taking in the pleasant fragrance of the bright coloured flowers and the newly grown lush wet leaves of the jam-packed garden. As he walked towards the old church, he felt the strange and wonderful feeling of godliness. The eternal feeling of eccentric spiritual supremacy that was completely new to him until now was bounded in his heart.

As soon as he entered the desolated church, his anxiety, fear, and sadness shrunk to his feet. His breaths lengthened and slowed concurrently as he walked up to the other end. On reaching his destination, he stood next to the empty lectern that had a pile of dust lying on it. His attempts to speak out loud and clear failed as his words were suppressed by the sheer soreness in his heart.

Warm tears filled his helpless eyes as emotions overtook his strong ability to control them. Holding his hands together and bending his head low before the Lord, he fell on to his weak knees and sincerely pleaded for Troniya's recovery. As he closed his swollen eyelids, the welled-up tears weakly plunged down and splashed against the old wooden floor that was illuminated by the yellowish-golden rays of the evening sun.

For several seconds, tears kept falling, drop by drop, and the dust that erupted from the wooden floor instantaneously vanished into the surrounding thin air.

At the end of his plea, he also promised he'd observe a fast for one whole day, which he honestly did the very next day. It was, in fact, a miracle when Edy heard from Mable about Troniya's miraculous quick recovery on the following day. He was overjoyed when he realized how quickly the Lord had taken his prayer into consideration. He thanked the Lord Almighty wholeheartedly and with utmost gratefulness.

Of course, aren't the most sincere prayers answered first?

On the evening before the last end-of-term exam, Edy was struck by the thought that Troniya loved reading poems. It was, according to his plan, the best way to express how much he loved her. Even without bothering about the difficult level of the following day's exam, he spent the entire two hours of preparation time for writing a poem which, he strongly believed, could change Troniya's opinion on him.

Page after page, he wrote and tore and wrote again.

'What do you think you're doing?' Barrie snorted after Edy had torn off the sixth page.

'Poem,' Edy said, deliberately tearing off another page off his empty book, 'she loves to read poems.'

'So?' Barrie anxiously asked, 'How is writing a poem going to help?'

'I just want her to know how much I love her.'

'You think writing a love poem would convince her?'

Edy looked at Barrie, for the first time since their conversation started. He thought, for a minute, about what Barrie had said. 'I'll only pray that it does,' he said and continued scribbling on a new, empty page.

At the end of the two-hour prep, Edy finally had one neatly written poem on a neat unruled paper.

Barrie, who had been constantly worrying about Edy wasting his preparation time, took in his hands the poem that Edy had written since the beginning of the prep. He read:

Endless Seas were the ill-fated Graves,
Deserted Beaches and Reddish Salty Waves,
Yards of Wine, what the Kingdom now Craves,

Rizlandia, Once the Symbol of Eternal Peace,
Avoided all the Weaponry and the Grease,
Vicious Kings came along the Western Breeze,
Elms had begun to shed their Golden-Brown Leaves,
Nevertheless, Thousands were sacked and left to Freeze,
Digging out Jewellery, including those of the queens,
Edging out thousands and thousands of immortal souls,
Never had they altered any of their routine roles.

Love had been Lost, Lost along with Old Goals,
Overcame several hurdles that changed their Vows,
Vicarious hunger revealed Millions of Empty Bowls,
Entangled were the post-apocalyptic Warrior Souls,
Scandalous wills of enemy pushed many to the Gallows.

Tranquillity soon faded on the Enemy Borders,
Raged Rizlandians' the Ravaging Riders,
On their Seas they Sailed like the Deadly Cursers,
None were spared by the Firing Metal Cannons,
Industrious Kingdom was down to Grey Ashes,
Yolk and Yeast, the Loot from those with Lashes,
Acrimonious temper, the vicious reason that Crushes.

Belligerence, a Blooming Bud in their Boiling Blood,
Aggression was the sole changer of their Cud,
Inevitable Anguish, a part of Life, like Worms to Mud,
Known world turned Pungent, Cruel, and Bloody Red,
Infidelity had swept Faith like the Great Flood,
Sleighs of Love and Hope, A gift long Dead,
Hasty Resolutions was a deadly mutant of their Buds,
Huddling Humanity bore a mark that Forever Bled.

Sigh. Barrie let out a deep sigh at the end of the last line.

'This is not even related,' Barrie whined. 'How did you think you could express your love with this poem?'

'It's hidden,' Edy said.

'You are out of your mind,' Barrie continued, dumping the poem onto the desk, not paying attention to what Edy was saying. 'You have lost it. God, please help him to get back his senses.'

Edy sat still, looking at the wall ahead of him.

'Are you even listening to me?' Barrie cried. 'I'm going to tear this page off so you can start to concentrate on tomorrow's exam.'

In a split second, Edy grabbed the poem from his bench mate. He calmly placed the page on the desk and pointed his finger to the first letter of every line. Barrie followed.

'EDY RAVENDEN LOVES TRONIYA BAIKISHH,' he read.

And read again and again and again. The third time Barrie had finished reading the first letter of every line vertically, he froze on his seat. His eyes stared at the shuddering page that contained the poem.

'Barrie?' Edy called out. 'Say something.'

There was a long silence on Barrie's end before he said, 'I don't know what to say.' He whispered, his eyes still going up and down along the vertical line. 'I sincerely pray that she gets to read this one.'

*   *   *   *   *   *

It was the last working day at MPS. The two-hour exam flew by at an unbelievable pace. At one in the afternoon, all the four-hundred-odd students of MPS were seen thronging out of the examination hall. In no time, everyone except Edy was back in the dorms, packing their belongings for the two-month-long break. It was the end of yet another year at one of the most renowned schools around.

Edy, who was standing at the entrance of the seniors' corridor now had all his hopes deteriorated.

Troniya had informed the others that she was moving out and that she hadn't had a clue as to which city her dad would be posted to. All she knew was the fact that she was, beyond doubt, moving out of the school and that was all that Edy knew. It was, by far, the most horrible news that Edy had gotten.

The huge metal gates of MPS opened to let in the first vehicle. It was a small minivan, already loaded with huge baggage and two large suitcases. Everyone at MPS knew that the first vehicles that came in had the most distance to cover. As the minivan stopped in the parking bay, Edy could see a recognizable man get out of it—Troniya's dad. He now had a French beard on and looked as tidy and organized as always. As he made his way towards the doorway of the girls' dormitory, he was greeted by his younger daughter, later by Troniya. For the first time in about a month, Edy could finally see a smile on her. He stood far away from their view and watched as the minivan was reloaded with two more huge suitcases.

The engine of the minivan roared as the driver started the van. They were all set to hit the highway. Edy felt his pocket that contained the two gifts that he was only hoping to give her. The plan had failed like always. The minivan started to move, and suddenly time around him passed in slow motion. The tinted glass of the van prevented outsiders from seeing the insides of the van. Edy's heart pounded ever weakly as the van picked up its pace.

The strong spring winds blew across the open fields of the school. The dried petals of the rain trees in the assembly ground fell off the branches and swirled according to the wind's direction.

Edy fixed his gaze on the window of the side door that Troniya was seen stepping into. He tried hard to see anything at all. The black reflective glass that reflected the bright sunrays obstructed the one last glimpse that he wanted to have, as nothing of the insides was visible.

The further the van got, the weaker his heartbeats grew. Dust erupted from the arid grounds and a miniature whirlwind emanated far ahead from the dry sand. He fetched the two gifts from his right trouser pocket and loosely held on to them. The van raced out of the dark-red metal gates, and the sound of the engine faded away into the lengths of the endless highway.

Edy's heart was at its weakest. By now he had lost all his mental strength and he plunged onto the muddy floor, still not talking his eyes off the opened school gates directly opposite to the seniors' corridor. The two limply held gifts trembled from the impact of the plunge. Tears filled his gazing eyes as he cried within.

The winds grew stronger and ruffled his messy hair. He raised his hand and the heart-shaped cup and the tiny love book were revealed in front of his grief-struck eyes.

The words on the side of the coffee cup shone from the sun's glittering rays. They looked hazy from the filled-up tears. A weak wink and the excess water rolled down, making the words, which he already knew by heart, more clearly visible and he wordlessly read along, 'Loving Is More Fulfilling Than Being Loved'.

* * * * * *

The Cruel Reminiscence

Monday, 03 June 2007

On the third of June, a cloudy day, Morey's Public School reopened for the commencement of a new academic year—2007. A surprising lot of the students had passed with flying colours from the previous year's end-of-term exams. Though all the credit went to Mr Joseph for implanting the unusual kind of seriousness and studiousness in the minds of the students, which did have an exceedingly positive impact on the overall results of the pupils, he, however, was not around to be thanked for his tiring effort.

Mr Joseph Matthew had quit the principal's post the following year. Not many knew the true reason behind his resignation, but some including Miss Ashria Kaum and Mr Hal believed that he had taken up retirement. The management, however, after having failed to convince

Mr Joseph to stay back, had to recruit a new principal for the post. That was when Dr Alexander White took over as the new principal of Morey's Public School.

Dr Alexander White was, like most principals, old, tidy, and organized. He was relatively short and comparatively less stern-looking than the previous principal. This leniency aspect was largely interpreted by the students when they saw a broad smile on him during the first assembly of the academic year. He had dark grey hair, greyer than that of Mr Joseph—an indication that he was not below sixty. His matching grey moustache was probably yet another funny aspect that he had on him, which added to his lenient-looking character.

A very tiny number of new students and teachers were seen during the school assembly—a serious indication that Dr White did not have as many serious testimonies as Mr Joseph Matthew had.

The classes quickly resumed after the first school assembly ended with Dr White's first speech that did not include a warning message at the end of it. The first benchers' group, which now consisted of Edy, Barrie, Jade, Allen, Celia, and Mable, was back to continue in grade 11. Mr Hal was appointed the class coordinator for grade 11 for the ongoing academic year. Fortunately or unfortunately for Edy, the students of grade 11 were allotted the same classroom that was allotted to them the previous year, making it all the more painful for him to spend the many days ahead as the memories from the previous year rushed back to him instantaneously.

The 'morning sadness' syndrome that he had been experiencing for quite some months reached its peaks as soon as he stepped into the classroom. His mind froze and thoughts turned glacial. Nothing could revive him from the clutches of his mental agony. Disturbing reminiscences came back to him uncontrollably—a lethiferous act that affected him like the plague.

After taking his old seat at row 1, desk 1, Edy languidly turned towards row 4, desk 3. There were two new girl occupants at the infamous desk. The mystic feeling that had swaddled his heart all the while when Troniya was around had long perished. His life at MPS, as he could feel, was perspicuous no more.

Thirty of the forty-eight had opted to stay at MPS to continue grade 11. The others had moved out to other colleges, while eight new students joined in.

After Barrie had enquired, Mable revealed that Troniya had not showed up in the dormitory.

'And are you sure that the number she had given wasn't working?' Barrie asked.

'I have been trying ever since the holidays began,' Mable promptly replied.

'Looks like her dad changed his cell number before we could get to her' Allen said.

'That's more like it,' Celia said, 'which is why the recorded computer voice always said, "The number you have dialled is temporarily out of service."'

Edy had already known that the number was not temporarily but permanently out of service.

'But why would she not have called up anyone?' Allen questioned.

'Considering all the ill things that has happened to her, she would probably want to forget everything about MPS,' Mable said, 'like we all try and forget a scary nightmare.'

'Or probably she lost all her contacts,' Barrie quickly said and looked at Mable as if to seriously say, 'You are not helping with that probable explanation of yours.'

'Are you telling me that nobody has a clue as to where Troniya is?' Jade said, to which Mable and Celia shook their heads in reply.

'She might probably join late,' Allen said. 'It isn't new that some students come late a week or two for personal reasons.' But nobody was sure if that was the case with Troniya.

'Or we could check with Miss Ashria Kaum,' Jade suggested. 'She can look into the register records for grade 11 and check if Troniya's name is registered.'

'That is a good idea,' Celia said.

Edy hurriedly approached Miss Ashria Kaum, who in return promised to get back to him with the register details after the meeting that she was to have with the new principal Dr White.

The classes commenced as Mr Hal started off with the induction process—a process to get the newcomers familiar with the rules and regulations of the institution.

After an agonizing two hours of waiting, Miss Ashria Kaum, revealed that Troniya's name hadn't been registered in the grade 11 records. As Edy heard the awful news, the ground below him sank to a bottomless pit. All the atrocious deeds that had led to the preventable disaster, including those of Ivan, Eric, Ray, Mr Joseph, and the inspecting squad members rewound from his memory like a damaged tape recorder.

An unblest fate had changed his life from what it always used to be to something that was never expected to be. Edy sat at his desk, unresponsive to everything that was going on around him. He largely looked like he was suffering from catatonia. The thought that Troniya was no more a part of MPS and no more an essential part of his routine life had left a blemishing effect on his philosophy and the purpose of his overturned life.

'Edy?' Barrie called out while the other first benchers' group mates watched helplessly. 'You okay?'

'Edy, say something,' Celia worriedly pleaded.

'I know it's hard for you right now . . . but—' Barrie stopped and languidly shook his head before bending low. He hadn't had a clue as to what might convince his best pal to get back his normality.

At row 1, desk 3, Jeoff had had a newcomer as his bench mate. He always felt excited about talking to the new ones and questioning about all that the newcomer did in their previous school. Likewise, Jeoff also loved to explain to the newcomers all the unusual things that the students did at MPS.

'Then we have the SSL,' Jeoff said to his new friend, 'Which stands for students' secret language.'

'Students' secret language?' the newcomer curiously asked.

Jeoff nodded and wrote down on the new empty book that he had placed on his desktop 'TBGDPRB WP RPMBZ'X OVEGJD XDKPPG'.

'How do I decode it?' the newcomer excitedly enquired. 'How do I read those letters?'

'Very simple,' Jeoff said and quickly wrote again, right below the SSL sentence.

| F - A |
| E - B |
| D - C |

| R - M |
| Q - N |
| P - O |

| L - G |
| K - H |
| J - I |

| X - S |
| W - T |
| V - U |

| Y - Z |

'Read A as F, B as E, C as D, so on and vice versa,' Jeoff explained. 'We call these the Sacred Secret Squares.'

'Wow,' the newcomer exclaimed and began decoding Jeoff's earlier sentence.

'WELCOME TO MOREY'S PUBLIC SCHOOL,' the newcomer wrote down after having decoded the sentence, using the Sacred Secret Squares.

'It's so simple,' the newcomer said, being excited at the secret language.

'Like I said, cakewalk for those who know it, but rocket science to those who don't,' Jeoff revealed. 'All you have to do is to remember those five secret squares.'

Edy, who had been listening to the conversation between Jeoff and his new companion, all of a sudden began to rummage in his desk.

The first benchers watched curiously as Edy thoroughly searched book after book. Finally, in the thick book that was at the bottom of the arranged column of books was a neatly folded sheet of paper.

'What on earth could possibly cheer him up in an instant?' Barrie endlessly thought at Edy's sudden change of mood.

The sheet was now in Edy's hands, and he fondly unfolded it before carefully placing it on top of his desk.

Barrie craned his head forward. Jade and Allen followed.

'What's this?' Jade asked. 'Looks like an SSL conversation.'

'It is,' replied Allen, who was indulgently decoding the message along with Barrie.

'You had an SSL conversation with Troniya?' Barrie questioned in surprise.

Edy dimly smiled and nodded in reply as he too decoded the last sentence of the SSL conversation.

'Good things come to those who wait,' he smilingly read out the last sentence. Allen, Barrie, and Jade looked on.

The last sentence by Troniya now began to spawn an undying efficacy of belief that implanted the seeds of a fresh hope in him.

'But it's just a—' Allen began, and before he could finish his potentially demoralizing sentence, Barrie stopped him and gave a fretful 'Shut up, will you?' look.

Barrie knew that the SSL conversation, though it certainly was not in the slightest degree an assured way to get back Troniya to MPS, was at least the last hope that could keep Edy's spirit up and going. At this stage Barrie understood how important it had become for Edy to believe so strongly in something—something that very remotely had anything to bring back his love.

'I will wait, Troniya,' Edy, whose buried hopes returned to life in a jiffy, thought to himself.

'*I will wait.*'